"If you apologize again, I'll slug you." Zora glared at Lucky.

He laughed, an unexpected rumble that rolled right into her heart. "That's my Zora." A bout of hard breathing reawakened the hope he might finally kiss her, but instead he sucked in a gulp of air and held it. "Okay. Better."

"Better than what?"

He ignored the question. "Since I inveigled you into working today, let me buy you lunch to celebrate."

"You're on." The heat in her body hadn't exactly dissipated, but it had faded into her normal pregnancy-enhanced high temperature. As for Lucky, clearly he didn't, couldn't and never would accept Andrew's babies as his own.

As common sense reasserted itself, Zora was suddenly glad nothing had happened. Going any further would have been yet another in a long line of mistakes she'd made with men. Gathering her possessions, she waited until Lucky locked up, and they sauntered out together. Friends again, nothing more.

Which was obviously how they both preferred it.

Dear Reader,

My heroine, ultrasound technician Zora Raditch, evolved as a supporting character during the past few Safe Harbor Medical romances. Wait! You don't have to read the other novels; each can stand alone. But it's been fun as well as challenging for me as an author to witness her growth from a husband-stealing pariah to a woman overcoming a broken heart and finding a real, lifelong love.

By coincidence, male nurse Luke (Lucky) Mendez entered the series in the same book (*The Baby Jackpot*), although I had no idea he and Zora would ultimately fall in love. They were enemies, with Lucky strongly disapproving of her past behavior. When they became housemates in *A Baby for the Doctor*, they were barely speaking to each other.

Both Zora and Lucky must confront past mistakes and rise above their flaws. Neither was a character I would have picked initially to take center stage, but here they are, having caught hold of my emotions until I could no longer resist them. I hope you'll find that you can't, either.

You can find more information about the series along with recipes mentioned in the past few books on my website, jacquelinediamond.com. Welcome to Safe Harbor, or welcome back!

Best,

Jacqueline Diamond

THE BABY
BONANZA

JACQUELINE DIAMOND

HARLEQUIN® AMERICAN ROMANCE®

Recycling programs
for this product may
not exist in your area.

ISBN-13: 978-0-373-75560-8

The Baby Bonanza

Copyright © 2015 by Jackie Hyman

Printed in U.S.A.

The daughter of a doctor and an artist, **Jacqueline Diamond** has been drawn to medical themes for many of her more than ninety-five published novels, including her Safe Harbor Medical miniseries for Harlequin American Romance. She developed an interest in fertility issues after successfully undergoing treatment to have her two sons, now in their twenties. A former Associated Press reporter and columnist, Jackie lives with her husband of thirty-five years in Orange County, California, where she's active in Romance Writers of America. You can learn more about her books at jacquelinediamond.com/books and say hello to Jackie on her Facebook page, JacquelineDiamondAuthor.

Books by Jacqueline Diamond

Harlequin American Romance

Safe Harbor Medical

His Hired Baby

The Holiday Triplets

Officer Daddy

Falling for the Nanny

The Surgeon's Surprise Twins

The Detective's Accidental Baby

The Baby Dilemma

The M.D.'s Secret Daughter

The Baby Jackpot

His Baby Dream

The Surprise Holiday Dad

A Baby for the Doctor

The Surprise Triplets

Visit the Author Profile page
at Harlequin.com for more titles

Chapter One

It was the first time Zora could recall agreeing with Lucky Mendez about anything. Although their truce surely wouldn't last long, she appreciated his good judgment this once.

"No way are you letting that creep move into our house," the male nurse told their landlady and housemate, Karen Wiggins. With his striking dark hair, muscular build and flamboyant tattoos, Lucky made an odd contrast to the pink streamers festooning their den.

"Everybody hates Laird Maclaine," Zora added as she arranged baby shower prizes on a side table. Being seven months pregnant with twins, she had to avoid any strenuous activity. In fact, as one of the shower's honorees—along with two of their former housemates—she could have dodged setup duty, but she refused to take the easy way out.

Ever.

"He's the only one who responded to the notice I posted on the bulletin board." Atop a step stool, Karen tied a bunch of balloons to a hook. In shades of pink and purple, each balloon proclaimed: Baby!

"We have a vacant room and the rent's almost due," she continued. "It's either Laird, or I post on the internet and we fend off the loonies. Unless you guys can produce another candidate, fast."

Lucky hadn't finished castigating the topic of the conversation. "One drink and Laird's telling raunchy jokes. Two drinks and he's leering at any lady who walks by." His lip curled. "Three drinks and we call the police."

"For a staff psychologist, he doesn't have a clue about how decent people act," Zora threw in.

"I don't care for him, either, but there are bills to pay." Karen, a financial counselor at Safe Harbor Medical Center, where they all worked, had inherited the five-bedroom home from her mother the previous December. Forced to take out a loan to repair the run-down property, she'd advertised for roommates. The arrangement had worked well despite the diverse personalities who'd signed on.

So far, three of the women had become pregnant, but the other two had married and moved out, unlike Zora. There was little chance she would marry the father of her babies, because he was already married. He was also her ex-husband, with whom she'd foolishly and, just before finalizing their divorce, trustingly had sex in the belief that her on-again, off-again high school sweetheart still loved her.

Zora rested her palm on her bulge, feeling the babies kick. How ironic that she'd gotten pregnant by accident at the worst possible time, after she and Andrew had tried for more than a year to conceive. They'd been on the point of seeking fertility treatments when she'd discovered he was cheating on her.

"We have plenty of other colleagues," Lucky persisted. "You guys are in a better position to meet them than me, since my office is out in the boonies." Lucky worked in the medical office building adjacent to the hospital.

"I've tried, but... Oh, yuck!" Karen broke off as a breeze through the rear screen door carried a fetid whiff of decomposing vegetation and fish from the estuary behind the property.

Zora nearly gagged, too. Karen praised the marsh ad

nauseum because it provided critical habitat for plants and small animals, as well as for California's migratory birds. However, despite the cooling weather at the end of September, it stank. "Who left the door open?"

"I must have forgotten to close it after I swept the patio." Lucky shut the glass slider with a thump. "How about renting to that receptionist in your office?"

"She declined." Descending from the stool, Karen stood back to assess the position of the balloons. "She prefers to save money by living with her parents. Speaking of money, if we don't find anyone by next month, I'll have to divide the room rent among you guys and Rod."

Their fourth and newest housemate, anesthesiologist Rod Vintner, had gone to pick up the party cake. He'd also gone, in Zora's opinion, to avoid anything approaching hard labor, although he *had* promised to clean up afterward.

"We could use the spare room as a nursery." Lucky cast a meaningful gaze at Zora's large belly. "If someone would inform her ex-husband that he's about to be a father and owes child support, she could afford the extra space."

"Don't start on her," Karen warned, saving Zora the trouble. "Go set up the chairs in the living room."

"Yes, ma'am." With a salute, Lucky strolled off. Zora tried to ignore the muscles rippling beneath his T-shirt and the tight fit of his jeans. The man was a self-righteous pain in the neck, no matter how good he looked.

Surprisingly, he hadn't brought home any dates since they'd moved into the house last February. Or none that she'd observed, Zora amended. Since Lucky occupied the downstairs suite, he could easily slip someone in late and out early without the others noticing. Men did things like that.

"You can stop staring at his butt now," Karen said dryly.

"I wasn't!"

"You can lie to anyone else, including yourself, but

spare me." The older woman—forty-two to Zora's twenty-
nine—tightened the ponytail holder around her hair, which
she'd dyed black this month. "Was that the kitchen timer?"

"I didn't hear anything." Zora adjusted a gift-wrapped
box with a slot for envelopes. The front read: Nanny Fund.
They planned to share the services of a specialist nanny
among the three new moms and their collective total of
six infants. Well, they *did* work at a hospital noted for its
fertility treatments, although only one of the pregnancies
had high-tech origins.

The timer buzzed. "There!" Karen said with satisfaction. "I knew it would sound any second."

"You must be psychic." Zora waddled behind her past a
table displaying shower-themed paper plates and napkins.

"I have a well-developed sense of when food is done.
Call it experience." In the kitchen, Karen snatched pot
holders from a hook and opened the oven, filling the air
with the scents of orange and lemon, almonds and bal-
samic vinegar.

Karen set the tins of Mediterranean muffins on the
stove to cool. "I'd better start on the finger sandwiches.
Only two hours before the guests are due, and I have to
dress." She tied an apron over her blouse and long, casual skirt.

"I'll finish the vegetables." From the refrigerator, Zora
removed the containers of celery, carrots and jicama that
she'd cut up earlier, along with sour cream to mix for the
dip and peanut butter to fill some of the celery sticks.
"Would you get the olives and an onion soup packet from
the pantry? I'm too big to squeeze in there."

"Gladly." Karen angled her slender shape around the
narrow bend that led to the storage area. "Just black olives, or green ones, too?"

"Both." Zora lowered herself onto a chair, grateful she
could still reach the table around her abdomen. A railing
underneath allowed her to prop up her swollen ankles, but

nothing alleviated the strain on her lower back. It ached more each day.

She hid her discomforts, determined to continue working as long as possible. Being an ultrasound tech meant standing on her feet all day and angling her midsection so she could scan the patients, but she was saving her paid maternity leave for after the twins' birth. Two months left—if they didn't arrive early.

After retrieving the requested items, Karen spread out her sandwich fixings on the counter. Through the kitchen's far door, Zora heard the scrape of folding chairs being opened and placed around the front room. She respected Lucky's work ethic; he always pitched in with an upbeat attitude. If he could only master the art of minding his own business, he'd be...well, tolerable.

Footsteps thudded on the carpet, announcing Lucky's return. His short, military-style haircut emphasized the strong planes of his face, which reflected his Hispanic heritage. "Where are the chair covers hidden? Someone else stored them after Anya and Jack's wedding."

"Upstairs in the linen closet," Karen said.

"Can I ride the stair lift or is that only for mommies?" Lucky teased. Both women narrowed their eyes at him, and he lifted his hands in a yielding gesture. "Just asking."

"Go play somewhere else," Zora muttered.

"Alone? That's no fun." With a rakish grin, he dodged out.

"You two should swap rooms so you could be downstairs," Karen observed from the counter. "Let him ride the stair lift if it gives him a thrill."

"I can't afford the extra rent." Lucky's large room commanded a correspondingly larger price. While Zora didn't care about having a personal patio exit, she did envy him the private bath. Karen had one, too, upstairs in the master suite, while Zora shared a bathroom with Rod and Melissa.

Or, rather, with Rod and whoever moved into the room Melissa had vacated when she'd remarried her ex-husband.

Some people have all the luck. A sigh escaped Zora. Too late, she tried to cover with a cough.

"A pickle chip for your thoughts," Karen said.

"No, thanks." Zora popped a black olive into her mouth.

"You really are entitled to support," Karen observed. "I wonder whether you'd have faced your ex by now if Lucky weren't such a nag."

"He has nothing to do with it."

"You're stubborn," was the reply. "Seriously, Zora, how long can you keep this secret? I'm amazed Andrew's mother hasn't spilled the beans."

"Betsy doesn't know." Zora's former mother-in-law was the nursing supervisor at the hospital. The kind-hearted lady had suffered through the loss of two beloved daughters-in-law, thanks to her son's faithlessness.

Zora wondered whether Betsy was being more cautious about bonding with Andrew's third wife, a Hong Kong native he'd met on a business trip while he was married to Zora. Unexpectedly, tears blurred her vision. *How could he cheat on me? And then, just when I was ready to let him go, trick me into believing he still loved me?*

"Betsy sees you in the cafeteria every day," Karen reminded her.

"She's aware that I'm pregnant," Zora agreed. "But she has no idea who the father is."

Karen stuck a hank of black hair behind her ear. "She isn't stupid."

"But I doubt she believes Andrew is capable of...of being such a grade-A jerk." Damn those tears stinging her eyes again. "Aside from my closest friends, most people accept my explanation that I made a mistake after my divorce. I let them assume I picked up a guy in a bar."

"And that's better than admitting you slept with Andrew?"

"It's better than admitting I'm a complete chump."

More footsteps, and Lucky reappeared. "They aren't there. Let's skip the seat covers."

"I refuse to have guests in my house sitting on ugly folding chairs," Karen said.

The man tilted his head skeptically. "What's the big deal? People have been sitting on folding chairs without covers since the dawn of time."

"No, they haven't." Hastily, Zora shielded the relish tray from his attempt to grab a carrot. "Hands off!"

"Evidence found in caves throughout northern Europe indicates that Neanderthals shunned folding chair covers as a sign of weakness," Lucky said. "And why so stingy with the veggies?"

"I'm still arranging these. Go eat a corn chip." Zora indicated a bag set out to be transferred into a large bowl.

"I'm a vegetarian."

"Corn is a vegetable."

"Corn chips do not occur in nature," he responded. "Just one carrot. Pretty please."

She flipped it toward him. He caught it in midair.

"Try the closet in my bathroom for the covers," Karen suggested to Lucky. "Top shelf."

"I have permission to enter the inner sanctum?" he asked.

"It expires in sixty seconds."

"Okay, okay." He paused. "Before I run off, there's one little thing I should mention about today's guest list."

Zora released an impatient breath. "What?"

"I invited Betsy."

"You didn't!" Keeping her ex-mother-in-law in the dark at work was one thing, but around here the babies' paternity was no secret.

Karen turned toward Lucky, knife in hand. "Tell me you're joking."

He grimaced. "Sorry. Spur-of-the-moment thing. But

your motto *is* the more the merrier, and besides, Betsy's a widow. If she's interested in renting a room, that would solve all our problems." With a carroty crunch, off he went.

"Unbelievable," Karen said.

If she hadn't been so huge, Zora might have given chase. She could easily have strangled Lucky at that moment. But then they'd have to find *two* new housemates.

"I'd say the cat's about to claw its way out of the bag," Karen observed. "Might as well seize the bull by the horns, or is that too many animal metaphors?"

"Considering the size of the rat we live with, I guess not," Zora growled.

Karen smiled. "Speaking of rats, if you'd rather not confront Andrew-the-rodent yourself, don't forget you can hire Edmond to do it." Edmond Everhart, their former roommate, Melissa's husband, had been Zora's divorce attorney.

"That'll only create more trouble." Zora scraped the onion dip from the mixing bowl into a container on the relish tray. "Andrew'll put me through the wringer."

"If that's your only reason for not telling him about the babies, I'd rate its validity at about a three on a scale of ten." Karen trimmed the crust from a sandwich.

Zora dropped the spoon into the mixing bowl with a clunk. "He's the only man I ever loved. I want to give him the benefit of the doubt."

"Zora, what benefit of what doubt?" Karen retorted. "He dumped you in high school, married someone else, then cheated on *her* with you after he ran into you at your class reunion. Let's not forget that he then cheated on *you* with what's-her-name from Hong Kong. Why on earth would you entertain the fantastical notion that Andrew will ever transform into a loving husband and father?"

With a pang, Zora conceded that that was exactly what she *did* wish for. While her rational mind sided with Karen, the infants stirring inside her with a series of kicks and squirms obviously missed their father. So did Zora.

"It can happen," she said. "Look at Melissa and Edmond. Three years after their divorce, they fell in love again."

"They'd quarreled about having children. Neither of them cheated on the other," Karen persisted. "Andrew can't be trusted, ever."

She spoke with the ferocity of a divorcée who'd survived an abusive marriage. It had taken more than a decade for Karen to trust a man again. She and their housemate, Rod, were still easing into their relationship.

"People can change." Despite a reluctance to bring up her family, Zora wanted Karen to understand. "Did I mention I have a twin?"

"Really?" Leaning against the counter, Karen folded her arms. "Identical or fraternal?"

"Identical." Zora wasn't about to reveal the whole story, just the important part. "But we quarreled, and we aren't in touch anymore. All I know of her is what Mom passes along." Their mother, who lived in Oregon, loved sharing news.

"Go on." After a glance at the clock, Karen resumed her food preparation.

"Nearly ten years ago, Zady ran off with a married man." Zora inhaled as deeply as she could, considering the pressure on her lungs from the pregnancy. "They live in Santa Barbara. He split with his wife and now he's devoted to Zady. They have a beautiful house and a couple of kids."

"Was there a wedding in there?" Karen asked dubiously.

"I'm sure there was, although she didn't invite me." The rift had been bitter, and there'd been no move toward reconciliation on either side. In fact, her mother said Zady had chuckled when she'd learned about Zora's divorce.

"So the guy married her, and you believe that if lightning struck your twin, it can strike you, too?" Karen murmured.

Zora's throat tightened. "Why not?"

"Because Betsy's about to arrive with her antennae on high alert. If I'm any judge, that woman's dying to be a grandmother."

"And she'll be a terrific one." The elder Mrs. Raditch did all the right grandmotherly things, such as baking and crocheting, a skill she'd taught Zora. "But…"

"You're running out of *but*s," Karen warned. "Unless you count Lucky's."

"I don't!"

"The way you guys battle, you're almost like an old married couple."

"We're *nothing* like a married couple, old or otherwise." Zora could never be interested in a man with so little class. Outside work, he flaunted his muscles in sleeveless T-shirts and cutoffs. While she didn't object if someone had a small tattoo, his body resembled a billboard for video games. On the right arm, a colorful dragon snaked and writhed, while on the left, he displayed a buxom babe wearing skimpy armor and wielding a sword.

Whenever she pictured Andrew, she saw him in the suit and tie he always wore as an international business consultant. He had tousled blond hair, a laser-sharp mind, sky-blue eyes, and when he trained his headlight smile on her, Zora understood why some poor fools became addicted to drugs, because the euphoria was irresistible.

At the image, vague intentions coalesced into a firm decision. "Andrew's the man I married. This…this *liaison* with what's-her-name is an aberration. Once the kids are born and he holds them in his arms, what man wouldn't love his own son and daughter?" *And their mother.*

Even Zora's own father, a troubled man who'd cheated on her mom, had stuck around while his kids had grown up. Well, mostly—there'd been separations and emotional outbursts that left painful memories. But there'd been tender times, too, including a laughter-filled fishing trip, and one Christmas when her father had dressed up as Santa Claus and showered them with gifts.

She longed for her children to experience a father like that. With Andrew's charm, he could easily provide such unforgettable moments.

For a minute, the only sound was the chopping of a knife against a cutting board as Karen trimmed crusts. Finally she said, "So you plan to hold it together until then, alone?"

"I have you guys, my friends." Zora struggled for a light tone. "All I have to do is stay on an even keel."

"Like a juggler tossing hand grenades on the deck of a sinking ship?" On a platter, Karen positioned sandwiches in a pyramid. "Well, it's your decision."

"Yes, and I've made it." Zora studied the relish tray through a sheen of moisture. Andrew would come around eventually. He had a good heart, despite his weak will.

"I'm happy to report that I found the chair covers and they look fine." Lucky's deep voice sounded almost in her ear, making her jump. "What do Neanderthals know, anyway?"

"Speaking of Neanderthals, how dare you sneak up on me?" she snapped. "I could go into labor."

"No, you won't." The corners of his mouth quirked.

"How would you know?"

"I'm a nurse, remember?" he said.

"Not that kind of nurse." He worked with a urologist.

"Pregnancy care is part of every nurse's basic medical training." His expression sobered. "Speaking of medicine, you're sure Cole's coming today?"

Dr. Cole Rattigan, the renowned men's fertility expert Lucky assisted, had been away this past week, speaking at a conference in New York.

"He and his wife RSVP'd," Karen assured him. "What's the big deal?"

"I can't discuss it. It concerns a patient."

"Why would you confer about a patient on your day off?" Zora asked.

"That's confidential, too." Grabbing the tray of sandwiches, Lucky whisked out of the room so fast it was a miracle the sandwich pyramid didn't topple.

"That's odd," Karen said. "I wonder what's going on."

As did Zora, but Cole, and in particular his wife, a popular nurse, were a touchy subject for her. As the first Mrs. Andrew Raditch, Stacy hadn't hidden her resentment toward Zora-the-husband-stealer, and most staffers had sided with her.

Among them, no one had been more hostile than Lucky. He'd eased up since he and Zora had started sharing this house, but in a showdown there was no question that his loyalty lay with Cole and his spouse.

Zora wished that didn't bother her. Well, she had more important things to deal with, anyway…such as facing the grandmother of her children in less than two hours.

Chapter Two

Lucky wove between clusters of chattering people in the living room, removing soiled paper plates and cups. Although he was enjoying the party, he wished he and his housemates had kept a tighter lid on the guest list. Only half an hour into it, the place was filling up—and not all the choices had been wise.

Inviting Betsy Raditch had seemed a clever trick to prod Zora into finally accepting the help she needed. Instead, the younger woman kept dodging her ex-mother-in-law, who sneaked longing gazes at Zora's belly but maintained a respectful distance. The would-be grandmother's wistful expression sent a guilty pang through Lucky.

And he hadn't counted on Karen inviting Laird, but here he was, fawning over Zora. The psychologist's colorless eyes—okay, they were gray, but a very *light* gray—lit up whenever she so much as flinched, providing an excuse for him to offer her a chair or a drink. Was the man flirting or just trying to charm his way into the house? Either way, he had a very strange notion of what women found appealing.

When Zora winced, the guy reached out to rub her bulge. Stuck in a knot of people across the room, Lucky barely refrained from shouting, "Hands off!" To his relief, Keely Randolph, a dour older nurse Lucky had never much liked until now, smacked Laird's arm and loudly proclaimed that people shouldn't shed their germs all over pregnant women.

After scowling at her, Laird gazed around, targeted Karen and approached her with a smarmy expression. Lucky caught the words *exquisite house* and *can't wait to move in*.

Rod Vintner came to Karen's rescue, his wiry frame and short graying beard bristling with indignation. "Who's moving in where?" he growled with a ferocity that indicated he'd willingly stick one of his anesthesiology needles into Laird's veins and pump it to the max.

Satisfied that the jerk was batting zero, Lucky glanced toward the front window. He never tired of the soul-renewing view across the narrow lane and past the coastal bluffs to the cozy harbor from which the town took its name. You couldn't beat the beauty of this spot.

Yet he might have to leave. And that had nothing to do with Laird or any other roommate.

Lucky had worked hard to earn a master's degree in nursing administration, which he'd completed earlier this year. Now he sought a suitable post for his management skills, but there were no openings at Safe Harbor Medical. Which meant he'd have to move away from the people he cared about.

They included Zora, who over the past few months had needed his protection as she struggled to deal with an unplanned pregnancy and a broken heart. They hadn't intended to grow closer; he wasn't even sure either would openly acknowledge it. Which was just as well. Because having once failed in a big way to be there for the people he loved, Lucky had vowed never, ever to take on such responsibility. Because he'd only fail again.

Still, he couldn't imagine moving away. His best hope for staying in the area would be the expansion of the men's fertility program in which he worked. Any minute now, its director, Cole Rattigan, would arrive. Most of the staff thought Cole had just been in New York to deliver a speech, but Lucky was more interested in hearing about his boss's private meeting with the designer of a new device.

It offered a slim possibility of helping one particular patient, a volatile billionaire named Vince Adams who was considering a major endowment to expand the hospital's urology program. If that happened, it might create a nursing-administration position for Lucky. Also, it would realize his doctor's dream of building a world-class program.

If not for Cole, Lucky might not be working for Safe Harbor Med at all, he reflected as he carried empty plates and cups to the kitchen. Two and a half years ago, when the newly arrived urologist had interviewed for office nurses, Lucky hadn't believed he had a chance of being hired. After his previous doctor retired, Lucky's tattoos had repeatedly knocked him out of the running for jobs. He'd been considering expensive and painful treatment to remove the evidence of his youthful foolishness.

But the tats hadn't bothered Cole. He'd asked a few questions, appeared pleased with the responses and offered the job on the spot. After that, Lucky would have battled demons if they'd threatened his doctor.

In the den, he poured himself a glass of fruit juice and noted that the sandwiches, chips and veggies were holding their own despite modest depletions. No one had cut the sheet cake yet, leaving intact the six cartoon babies, five with pink hair ribbons and one with blue.

"Aren't they adorable?" The soft voice at his elbow drew his attention to Betsy.

Lucky shifted uneasily. Despite his conviction that Zora ought to be honest with her children's grandmother, he had no intention of snitching. Still, he *had* invited the woman. "We ordered it from the Cake Castle."

She indicated the Nanny Fund box bordered by a few wrapped packages. "I didn't realize most people would be contributing money as their gift. I hope it's all right that I crocheted baby blankets."

"All right?" Lucky repeated in surprise. "The kids will treasure those keepsakes forever."

Betsy's squarish face, softened by caramel-brown hair and wire-rimmed glasses, brightened at the compliment. Why didn't Zora level with the woman? A doting grandma could provide the support a young single mother needed. Considering that Zora's own mother lived in Oregon, she'd be wise to take advantage of Betsy's yearning for grandkids.

"I'm glad to hear it," she said. "Also, much as I approve of the nanny idea, I suspect new mothers could use furnishings and toys."

"Oh, there's plenty of that." Lucky had been forced to park in the driveway for weeks due to the overflow in the garage. "Practically the entire staff has donated their baby gear. Anya and Jack got first pick, since she's already delivered, but they only have a singleton. There's plenty left."

"They're a lovely couple. So are Melissa and Edmond." Betsy indicated the long-legged blonde woman ensconced on the sofa, flanked by her doting husband and seven-year-old niece, Dawn, who lived with them. This was a rare outing for Melissa, who in her sixth month with triplets looked almost as wide as she was tall. "I'm thrilled that they remarried. They obviously belong together."

Was that a hint? Surely the woman didn't believe her son might reconcile with Zora. Aside from the fact that he had a new wife, the guy was the world's worst candidate for family man. "I'd bet in most divorces the odds of a happy reconciliation would be on par with winning the lottery."

"If that was for my benefit, don't bother," Betsy told him.

"Sorry." Lucky ducked his head. "I tend to be a mother hen to my friends. Or a father hen, if there is such a thing."

"At least you aren't a rooster like my son," she replied sharply.

"No comment."

"Wise man."

On the far side of the room, Zora circled past the staircase and halted, her eyes widening at the sight of Lucky standing beside Betsy. Lucky nearly spread his hands in a do-you-honestly-think-I'd-tell-her? gesture, but decided against it, since Betsy didn't miss much. She must be suspicious enough already about the twins' paternity.

While he was seeking another topic of conversation, his landlady bounced into the den from the kitchen. "Who's ready for a game?" Karen called. "We have prizes." She indicated a side table where baskets displayed bath soaps and lotions, while a large stuffed panda held out a gift card to the Bear and Doll Boutique.

"What kind of game?" Dawn asked from the couch.

"I'm afraid the first one might be too hard for a child," Karen said. "It's a diaper-the-baby contest."

"I can do that," the little girl proclaimed.

"Yes, she can," Melissa confirmed. "Dawn has more experience with diapering than Edmond or me."

"I used to help our neighbor," the child said.

"Then please join in!" Karen beamed as guests from the living room crowded into the den. "Ah, more players. Great!"

Among the group was their former roommate Anya, her arms around the daughter she'd delivered a few weeks earlier. "Nobody's diapering Rachel for a game."

"Certainly not," Karen agreed.

"However, volunteers are welcome to stop by our apartment any night around two a.m.," put in Anya's husband, Dr. Jack Ryder.

Rachel gurgled. A sigh ran through the onlookers, accompanied by murmurs of "What an angel!" and "How darling!"

"I'd be happy to hold her for you," Betsy said. "You can both relax and enjoy the food."

"Thank you." Anya cheerfully shifted her daughter into the arms of the nursing supervisor.

When Zora hugged herself protectively, Lucky felt a twinge of sympathy. She'd refused to consider adoption, declaring that this might be her only chance to have children, but the sight of little Rachel must underscore the reality of what she faced.

Children required all your resources and all your strength. How did this woman with slim shoulders and defiant ginger hair expect to cope by herself?

He reminded himself not to get too involved. Lucky didn't mind changing a few diapers, but he might not be here long, unless Dr. Rattigan brought good news. Now where was the doctor?

Waving a newborn-size doll along with a package of clean diapers, Karen detailed the rules of the game. "You have to remove and replace the diaper. I'll be timing you. Fastest diaper change wins."

"That doesn't sound hard," Laird scoffed.

"Did I mention you have to do it one-handed?" Karen replied, to widespread groans. "If you drop the baby on the floor, you're automatically disqualified."

"For round two, contestants have to diaper the doll blindfolded," Rod added mischievously. A few people laughed, while Dawn's jaw set with determination. That kid would do it upside down and sideways to win, Lucky thought. With that attitude, she'd go far in life.

Then he caught the sound he'd been waiting for—the doorbell. His pulse sped up. "I'll get it."

Someone else reached the door first, however, and friends rushed to greet the Rattigans. Despite his impatience, Lucky hung back.

With her friendly manner and elfin face, Stacy had a kind word for everyone. Her mild-mannered husband said little; Cole's reticence, Lucky knew, stemmed partly from the urologist's discomfort in social situations. It was also partly the result of having a brain so brilliant that he was probably carrying on half a dozen internal conversations with himself at any given moment.

Lucky could barely contain his eagerness to speak with the great man privately and find out if the device lived up to its promise. However, he drew the line at elbowing guests aside.

Stacy oohed over Anya's newborn and hugged Betsy, her former mother-in-law. The room quieted as the first Mrs. Andrew Raditch came face-to-face with the woman who had cheated with him before being discarded in turn. Most of the staff had cheered at Zora's misfortune, believing she was receiving her just deserts. Lucky was ashamed to admit he'd been among them. Now he wished he could spare her this awkwardness.

"Wow! Look at you." Stacy patted Zora's belly. "Have you chosen names yet?"

"Still searching," she said with a tentative smile. "For now, Tweedledee and Tweedledum."

This light exchange broke the tension. With her new marriage, Stacy had clearly moved on, and with her courtesy toward Zora, she'd brought her old nemesis in from the cold.

Silently, Lucky thanked her. Cole had chosen a worthy wife.

The game began, with guests lining up to participate. Seizing his chance, Lucky approached his boss, who spoke without prompting.

"I know you're anxious for news, Luke." Cole used Lucky's formal name. "Let's talk."

"We'll have more privacy in here." Lucky led the way into the now-empty living room.

ZORA HAD NO interest in diapering a baby. She'd be doing more than her share of that soon.

Stacy's display of friendliness left her both relieved and

oddly shaky. Having been treated as a pariah by much of the hospital staff for several years, Zora still felt vulnerable as well as guilty.

Also, Stacy's question about the names reminded Zora of her idea to leave the decision until they were born. She'd figured that if Andrew had a chance to choose the names, it might help bond him with the little ones. Today, however, the prospect of what lay ahead was sinking in.

For starters, what was she planning to do, call him from the delivery room and break the news of his paternity over the phone while writhing in agony? This kind of information should be presented in person, and she ought to get it over with now. Yet being around Andrew brought out Zora's weakness for him; the ease with which he'd seduced her when she dropped by with their divorce papers proved that.

If only Lucky would stop poking at her, she'd be able to think clearly. It might be unfair to focus her anger on her housemate, but this was none of his business. And why had he, one of the party's hosts, hustled Dr. Rattigan off in such a hurry?

Hungry as usual these days, Zora munched on a peanut butter–filled celery stick from the snack table. Keely drifted alongside, following her gaze as Lucky vanished. "Nice build," the older nurse observed in her nasal voice.

Amused, Zora said, "I don't believe he's dating anyone. Interested?"

Keely snorted. "Not my type."

Zora didn't dare ask what that was.

A hint of beer breath alerted her to Laird Maclaine's approach. The psychologist must have downed a brew before arriving, because they weren't serving alcohol.

"We're discussing Mendez?" He addressed his question to Zora, ignoring Keely. "If he snags a better job with that new master's degree of his, I'd love to rent *his* room. I hear it has an en suite bathroom."

"En suite?" Keely repeated. "What a pretentious term." Laird rolled his eyes.

"He isn't leaving." While Zora understood Lucky's desire for advancement, she couldn't imagine him abandoning his friends.

The psychologist shrugged. "Either way, this is a fantastic party house. I'm expecting to move in next weekend."

Astonished, Zora slanted an assessing gaze at the psychologist. From an objective viewpoint, Laird wasn't bad-looking, although bland compared to Lucky, and she respected him for initiating and leading patient support groups. But it would be annoying to have to run into this conceited guy every morning over breakfast and every night at dinner.

Impulsively, she addressed Keely. "We have an empty room that used to be Melissa's. Any chance you're interested?"

"It's taken, by me," Laird rapped out.

"Nothing's settled," Zora said.

"Don't you already have two men living here?" Keely inquired. "You and Karen should bring in another woman. I'd join you, but I couldn't do that to my roommate."

"You wouldn't fit in, anyway," Laird growled.

That remark didn't deserve a response. "Who's your roommate?" Zora asked Keely. "Do I know her?"

"Oh, she doesn't work at the medical complex," the nurse responded. "She's a housekeeper."

"I admire your loyalty to her."

"Anyone would do the same."

A stir across the den drew their attention. It was Dawn Everhart's turn at the game. Deftly, the little girl rolled the doll with an elbow, tugged on one diaper tab with her fingers and caught the other in her mouth, all while onlookers captured the moment with their cell phones.

"Unsanitary," Laird protested.

"But clever," Rod responded from his post beside Karen. "Besides, it's a doll."

"And she's beating the pants off everyone else's time," Edmond observed, beaming at his niece. "Literally."

Her feet having swollen to the size of melons, Zora wandered into the kitchen and sat down. Through the far door, she detected the low rumble of masculine voices in the living room.

What were Lucky and his boss discussing so intently? Had Cole made job inquiries at the conference for his nurse's sake? Although she'd instinctively dismissed Laird's comment about Lucky moving, the man couldn't be expected to waste his master's degree.

If Lucky departed, who would run out for ice cream when she had a craving? Lucky had promised to haul two bassinets and a changing table to the second floor as soon as she was ready for them. Without him around, who would cart her stuff up and down the stairs? She certainly couldn't count on Laird pitching in.

Well, she'd survive. In fact, she shouldn't be relying on Lucky so much, anyway. Zora hated to depend on others, especially someone so controlling and critical and arrogant and judgmental. She might not have the world's best taste in men, but she knew what she *didn't* like, and Lucky epitomized it. Now what were he and Dr. Rattigan talking about so intently?

No matter how hard she strained, she couldn't follow the thread of conversation from the living room. Just when she caught a couple of words, a burst of cheering from the den obliterated the rest of the doctor's comments.

Judging by the clamor, Dawn had edged out Anya's husband, Jack, by two seconds. "I can visualize the headline now—Seven-year-old Defeats Obstetrician in Diapering Contest!" roared Rod, who, as Jack's uncle, had the privilege of ragging him mercilessly. "I'm posting the pictures on the internet."

"You do that and you'll never see your great-niece again," Jack retorted. He spoiled the effect by adding, "Will he, cutie?" apparently addressing the newborn.

Zora lumbered to her feet. She was missing all the fun and worrying for nothing.

Probably.

Chapter Three

Feeling miles from the festivities in the den, Lucky struggled to concentrate on Cole's account. He kept wishing that, if he focused hard enough, the results would be more encouraging.

"The new stent won't fix what's wrong with Vince Adams." The slightly built doctor ran a hand through his rumpled brown hair.

"Are you certain?" Lucky pressed.

Cole nodded. "It won't do anything for a patient who has that much scar tissue."

During the summer, Cole had used the latest microsurgical techniques in an unsuccessful attempt to open the billionaire's blocked sperm ducts. As the office nurse, Lucky hadn't assisted at the operation, but he'd read the follow-up report. The procedure hadn't been able to reverse the extensive damage left by a long-ago infection.

However, Vince continued to press them for options. Cole had told him about a new dissolvable, medicine-infused stent, and Vince had been excited that Cole would get an advance preview of the device. "We have the world's top urologist right here," the millionaire had trumpeted. "And I'll be the first guy he cures."

The higher the hopes, the harder the fall.

"Do you think his interest in Safe Harbor is entirely based on restoring his fertility?" Lucky asked.

"It's hard to say," Cole replied. "His intentions tend to shift with his emotional state."

A private equity investor, Vince Adams was powerful and rich. But wealth hadn't compensated for his inability to sire children. Over the years, he'd paid dearly for treatments without success, and others had paid dearly for his desire for fatherhood.

After several turbulent and childless marriages, Vince had wed a woman with two young daughters. Determined to adopt them, he had used his financial clout to overwhelm Portia's first husband in court.

The man he'd gleefully trounced was Lucky's housemate, Rod Vintner, who'd faced a doubly devastating loss. First, during his divorce, he'd learned that his daughters were actually the genetic offspring of his unfaithful wife's previous lover, now out of the picture. Second, Rod had been outspent and outmaneuvered fighting for joint custody.

For years, he'd been forbidden to talk or even write to his daughters, who lived a ninety-minute drive away, in San Diego. Then, earlier this year, the older girl had run away from home. The twelve-year-old had contacted Rod, who'd enlisted the aid of the girls' maternal grandmother here in Safe Harbor.

Although officially Rod was still banned, Grandma Helen had arranged for Tiffany—now thirteen—and her younger sister to visit her more often. Whenever possible, she let them meet with Rod, and, faced with Tiffany's threats to run away again, the Adamses pretended not to notice.

Vince's search for fertility, however, provided him with another avenue for keeping Rod in line. While Vince's interest in the hospital stemmed in large part from his discovery that one of the world's foremost urologists had joined the staff, it also ensured that Rod didn't dare become too much of an annoyance. An anesthesiologist would be a lot easier for the hospital to replace than a billionaire donor.

Lucky hated that the staff had to curry favor with Vince. Still, he felt compassion for a man desperate to produce a baby. The billionaire's motives might be self-serving, but his comments had made it clear that he would treasure his child. As long as parents offered a loving, secure home, it wasn't anyone else's right to pass judgment.

However, if Cole couldn't help him, it seemed likely Vince wouldn't follow through on his major donation. "Suppose he drops us," Lucky said. "Surely there are others we could approach."

"The world is full of rich people, but Safe Harbor tends to lose out to more prestigious institutions," Cole responded. "I admit, Luke, being at the conference whetted my appetite for better research facilities, more lab space and money for fellowships. In fact, I received three excellent offers to relocate."

Lucky's heart nearly skipped a beat. "You'd take another position?"

Alarm flitted across the doctor's face. "I shouldn't have said that."

Nevertheless, he *had* said it. "If you go, the program will never recover." *Neither will I. On many levels.*

At a burst of laughter from the other room, Lucky flinched. His friends had no idea that he was standing here with the ground crumbling beneath his feet.

Cole's brow furrowed. "I joined Safe Harbor with the intention of building a standout program. Although I'm no longer sure that will be possible, this is my wife's home, and mine, too. I haven't given up yet." But there was no mistaking his distress.

"Nothing else at the conference might be useful?"

"I'm afraid not. Perhaps we should suggest Mr. Adams cancel next Saturday's appointment and save himself a trip." The billionaire tended to arrive with plenty of pomp and circumstance by private plane or helicopter. On other occasions, Vince roared up the coast in a high-performance car that cost as much as many houses.

If only Lucky could find a solution, for his sake and for his doctor's. It would also be important to the medical center to achieve its goal of becoming a major player in the fertility field. Major gifts attracted additional donors; a lack of progress might, by contrast, eventually consign Safe Harbor to secondary status. And this place had been good to Lucky when he'd needed help the most.

"Don't cancel," he said. "That's a week from now. Things could change."

"I suppose you're right." Cole stretched his shoulders. "In any event, my patient deserves to hear the news from me in person."

To Lucky, it was a reprieve. He had a week to figure out the next move.

ZORA HAD NEVER seen Lucky abandon a party before. After talking to Dr. Rattigan, he'd spent the next hour in a corner of the living room, fiddling with his phone. Searching the internet or texting people? But why?

In view of the doctor's wistful expression, it didn't take a genius to recognize that they'd suffered a blow. They must have been counting on the New York conference for some reason.

Zora tried to shrug off Lucky's absence while she and her fellow moms-to-be opened gifts. Most people had contributed money, but Betsy's gifts were special.

Zora's throat constricted as she held up the soft pink and blue blankets. Her former mother-in-law had created these precious heirlooms even without being sure of her relationship to the twins.

Zora was glad now that Lucky had invited Betsy. To learn she'd been excluded from the baby shower would have been an undeserved slap in the face.

Catching Betsy's eye, Zora said, "These mean more than I can say."

"I'm glad." Wedged among the other guests, the older woman added, "If you need anything, please call me."

"You're a sweetheart." But Zora wouldn't ask for the other woman's help, not until after the babies were born and she revealed the truth to Andrew. When she did, she hoped Betsy wouldn't resent having been kept in the dark.

Her gaze drifted to the diamond-and-emerald ring on her ex-mother-in-law's right hand. Zora had worn the family heirloom during her marriage, treasuring both its beauty and its significance. After the divorce, she'd returned it, with regret. Neither of Andrew's other wives had worn it; there'd been a special bond between Betsy and Zora that had begun in her high school days.

Now, its glitter reminded Zora of how much she'd lost. Not only her husband, but a woman who'd been as close to her as family. Well, perhaps someday she and Betsy could be close again.

She hoped her children would meet her twin sister, too. That depended on whether Zora was ever secure enough to handle Zady's inevitable gloating at her downfall. For now, distance was best. Nobody could inflict as much pain as the people nearest your heart.

After the last guest departed, the adrenaline that had powered Zora all afternoon faded. She collapsed on the living room couch while, inside her, the babies tussled.

What a blessing it would be when they were born and her body returned to normal. And what a joy to hold them and see their sweet faces.

At this point, Lucky should have arrived to offer her refreshments. She missed his coddling, even though it was often seasoned with criticism.

Instead, he bustled about collecting trash as if she weren't there. From the kitchen, Zora heard Karen opening and closing the fridge to put away food, while in the den, Rod ran the vacuum cleaner. Zora would have pitched in if she'd had the energy.

As Lucky removed the white linen covers from the folding chairs, his dark eyebrows drew together like storm clouds. The dragon protruding from beneath one sleeve appeared to be lashing its tail.

Zora broke the silence. "Won't you tell me what happened?"

He tossed a cover onto a pile of laundry. "What do you mean?"

"You've been upset since you talked to Dr. Rattigan."

Lucky snapped a chair shut. "Doesn't concern you."

Zora tried a different tack. "Laird speculated you might move out of town to take a better job. He's angling to get your suite." She deliberately baited Lucky with that reference to the obnoxious psychologist.

Lucky grimaced. "I'd rather not discuss that lowlife."

"Then let's discuss what's eating you."

"Like I said, it's none of your business."

Any second, flames were going to shoot out her ears. "Oh, yes, it is!"

"How so?" he growled, wielding a chair as if he was prepared to thrust it at her.

The guy sure was prickly. "It's obvious Cole brought bad news from the conference."

Lucky set the chair down. "I can't discuss anything involving a patient."

He was right to safeguard the man's privacy, Zora conceded. Medical personnel were required to do that, by law and by hospital policy as well as by simple decency. Still, he'd dropped a clue. Now, why would a patient's condition bother Lucky so much?

From the kitchen, Karen's voice drifted to her. "I'm looking forward to having your girls in town next Saturday. Should we invite them and Helen for lunch?"

"I doubt there'll be time," Rod replied dourly. "They're

only being dropped off at their grandma's for an hour or two while Vince sees his doctor."

"Is he having problems?" Karen asked. "I don't usually wish anyone ill, but he's an exception."

"You can wish that jerk as much ill as you like." Rod's voice rose in anger. "Tiff and Amber loathe the man. He may not physically abuse them, but he's a bully, and emotional scars can be the worst kind."

As the rumble of the garbage disposal cut off further eavesdropping, Zora put two and two together. Everyone knew—because the billionaire had discussed it openly—that Dr. Rattigan was treating him. And the men's program counted on his support.

"It's Vince Adams," she said. "No, don't answer. I realize you can't confirm it."

Lucky stacked the chairs to one side. "Are you still mad at me for inviting Betsy? Is that why you're harassing me?"

Zora tried to hug her knees, but her bulge was in the way. "I'm glad you invited her."

"So we're good?" His fierce brown eyes raked over her.

"No. What if you leave?" she burst out, surprised by her rush of emotion. "We're having enough trouble finding one roommate, let alone two. We'll *have* to take Laird."

A knot in her chest warned that she was less concerned about Laird than she was about Lucky staying until the babies were born. Until Andrew hopefully came to his senses and fell in love with his children. *Until hell freezes over.* No, but if hell did freeze over, she'd counted on Lucky to be there with a warming blanket.

As a friend, of course. He'd been just as helpful to Anya—maybe more so—when they'd moved into this house. It was in his nature.

Lucky stopped fiddling around. "You shouldn't upset yourself. It might shoot up your blood pressure."

"Then talk to me."

He plopped his butt on the arm of the couch. "About what?"

"You've been delving into your phone all afternoon, trying to find a solution, right? But if Dr. Rattigan can't fix Vince—I mean, Patient X—neither can you."

"So?" Lucky folded his arms. They were muscular arms, and he folded them across a broad, powerful chest. Too bad the movement also flexed the shapely legs of a cartoon woman, which rather spoiled the effect for Zora.

"We have to figure out another way to keep the Adamses involved with Safe Harbor," she blurted.

"We?" Lucky was addicted to monosyllables today.

She'd surprised herself by saying that. But didn't she owe Lucky a favor, considering how much support he'd given her?

"Yes, *we*," Zora retorted, and, to cut off any argument, she added, "Some people have a ridiculously hard time accepting help, to quote a person I know."

That produced a tight smile. "What do you imagine you, or we, can do regarding this alleged situation?"

"I have an idea." Fortunately, a possibility had hit her. "I'll share it on one condition." She might as well benefit from this.

"Which is?"

"You stop nagging me about my personal choices, however stupid you may consider them."

Lucky didn't answer. Then, abruptly, he burst out laughing. "Sometimes I actually like you."

"Why?" she asked suspiciously.

"Because you're a tough little cookie. If only you would apply that quality to he-who-shall-remain-nameless."

"That's breaking the rules," Zora retorted. "No nagging and no smart-aleck remarks, either. Well?"

"You're draining all the fun out of our relationship." Lucky raised his hands in mock surrender. "I agree. Now, what's the suggestion?"

The sight of him leaning close, intent on her, sent a thrill across her nervous system. Must be the maternal hormones running amok. "Remember when Edmond gave that speech about trends in family law?"

Melissa's husband served as a consultant for staff and patients on the legal aspects of fertility issues.

"Sure." Another one-syllable response.

"Afterward, Vince approached him for advice." Zora had heard the story from Melissa. Quickly, she added, "It was in a public place. No attorney-client privilege."

"Advice about what?"

"About persuading Mrs. Adams to agree to in vitro." If Vince produced even a small amount of sperm, it could be extracted and injected into an egg, bypassing the need to fix his blocked ducts. "She refuses to undergo in vitro, however."

"He can afford to hire a surrogate," Lucky pointed out.

"He objects to bringing in a stranger while his wife is presumably still fertile." Although Zora detested Portia for Rod's sake, she understood why a woman approaching forty wouldn't be eager to undergo a process involving hormone shots as well as uncomfortable procedures to harvest her eggs and implant the embryos. There were also potential health risks from a pregnancy complicated by multiple babies.

"What does this have to do with us?" Lucky asked.

"Talking to Edmond renewed Vince's enthusiasm for Safe Harbor." According to Melissa, the hospital administrator had phoned later to congratulate Edmond on saving the day.

"Renewed his enthusiasm how?" Lucky persisted. "His wife still hasn't agreed, as far as I know."

"I'm not sure, but judging by what Rod says about him, he enjoys power trips," Zora observed. "He hates to lose. If we figure out how he can win in this situation, it might keep him engaged with Safe Harbor."

"Any suggestions?"

"Ask Edmond what *he* advised."

Lucky considered this in silence. At close range, Zora noticed an end-of-day dark beard shadowing his rough cheeks. Although she preferred men with a smooth, sophisticated look, she had to admit there was something appealing about Lucky's male hormones proclaiming themselves loud and clear.

What was wrong with her? At this stage of pregnancy, she ought to have zero interest in sex. Or men. Or sexy men. Or... *Stop that.*

"Any idea which days Edmond's at the hospital?" Lucky asked.

"Afraid not."

In the adjacent dining room, Karen rose after stowing a tray in the sideboard. "Monday mornings and Thursday afternoons. Why the interest in Edmond?"

"It's private," Zora and Lucky said simultaneously.

Descending the few steps to the living room, their landlady gathered the pile of chair covers. "That's unusual, you guys being on the same page."

They both returned her gaze wordlessly until she sighed and departed. Zora chuckled. That had been fun.

Lucky held out his hand. As her fingers brushed his, a quiver of pleasure ran through her. On her feet, she lingered close to him for a moment, enjoying the citrus smell of his cologne underscored by masculine pheromones. Then in the recesses of her mind, she remembered something he often said: *it's Andrew who should be helping you, not me.*

Even without speaking, he projected criticism. Glowering, and ignoring Lucky's puzzled reaction, Zora headed for the stair lift.

Chapter Four

On Monday mornings while Cole performed surgeries at the hospital, Lucky replenished supplies, scheduled follow-up appointments with patients and prepared for office procedures in the afternoon.

He'd hoped to slip out to talk to Edmond, but the attorney was fully booked and could only spare a few minutes at lunch. It would have to do. But the morning turned out to be busier than expected, due to a special request from the fertility program director, Dr. Owen Tartikoff. A new urologist, a specialist in men's reconstructive surgery, would soon be joining the staff and Dr. Tartikoff needed someone to review the applications for his office nurse. Due to Lucky's administrative degree, Cole had recommended him.

Pleased at the responsibility, Lucky sifted through digital résumés to select the best candidates. The final choice would be left to the new physician, since the relationship between a doctor and his nurse was crucial. The right person eased the doctor's job, increased efficiency and decreased errors.

The wrong person could cause all sorts of unwanted drama. Hospital lore included a by-now-legendary clash between Keely Randolph and Dr. Tartikoff shortly after his arrival a few years ago. There'd been a spectacular scene when the abrasive Dr. T had dressed her down for an error and she'd blown up, calling him arrogant and egotistical before stalking out.

In view of her long history at Safe Harbor, she'd received a second chance with another obstetrician, Paige Brennan. Miraculously, the chemistry between them had proved stable rather than explosive. Keely spoke of her doctor in glowing terms, which in Lucky's view was how a nurse should behave.

He smiled, remembering how Keely had stood up for Zora at the party, staving off Laird's attempt to touch her. While his attentions hadn't necessarily been sexual, Lucky wouldn't put it past the man.

An image of Zora filled his mind as he recalled her unexpected offer to aid in his quest to expand the men's program. Her teasing grin was irresistible, and who would have imagined a mother-to-be could radiate such sexy vibes? True, she'd been cute before she got pregnant, but Lucky had been too caught up in resenting her for Stacy's and Cole's sakes to take more than a passing notice.

Not that there was any risk of a romance developing between him and Zora. He would never fall for anyone who led such a messy life, and he didn't appear to be her type, either. Judging by Andrew, she went for slick and manipulative, hardly adjectives that applied to a tattooed guy from a rough part of LA.

A guy who'd committed his share of mistakes and was determined not to repeat them, especially if a wife and children were at stake. If he were ever so blessed, Lucky vowed to be sure his family's circumstances were as close to perfect as humanly possible. He'd give them a financial buffer. A protective circle of love, commitment and security. If he couldn't be sure he could provide those things, he'd rather not risk marrying at all.

Lucky focused on the résumés on the computer screen. There were a number of nurses eager to work in such a prestigious environment with regular hours and benefits.

He struggled to view them through the perspective of an employer instead of as a fellow nurse who'd spent a year on his own job search. More than ever, he appreciated Cole's willingness to bring him on board.

Clicking open a new résumé, Lucky frowned in confusion. Was this a joke? Someone had inserted a slightly altered photo of Zora. Her face was narrower, but he'd recognize her anywhere.

Only the name on the file was Zady Moore. *Zady, huh?* He read on, prepared for humorous remarks, but the data seemed straightforward. This so-called Zady had grown up near Safe Harbor, just like Zora. Same age, too. In fact, same birth date.

She claimed to have a nursing degree and to work for a urologist in Santa Barbara, a couple of hours' drive north of here. Switching to the internet, Lucky confirmed that there was indeed a Zady Moore listed in connection with that urologist's office. If this was a hoax, someone had gone to great lengths.

The name Moore struck him as familiar. Oh, right. He'd seen mail addressed to Zora Moore Raditch.

Could Zora have a twin she'd never told him about? Or did she have a cousin with an eerily similar appearance and the same birth date?

The alarm on his watch shrilled, a reminder of his meeting with Edmond. Lucky set aside the résumé with several others marked for further consideration.

From the fourth floor, he took the stairs to the medical building lobby and strode out past the pharmacy into the late September sunshine. A salty breeze wafted from the ocean a mile to the south, while seagulls wheeled overhead.

Next door, the six-story hospital rose in front of him, a lovely sight with its curved wings. Remodeled half a dozen years earlier to specialize in fertility and maternity services, it had established a national reputation by hiring distinguished doctors such as Cole and Dr. T, and by adding state-of-the-art laboratories, surgical suites and equipment. As a result, the side-by-side buildings were bursting at the seams with staff and patients.

Lucky glanced across the circular drive at the vacant dental building that had been mired in bankruptcy proceedings. Once the bankruptcy judge allowed a sale, it would be snapped up fast. The corporation that owned Safe Harbor Medical Center had expressed interest in buying it, but had balked at the high price.

When Vince Adams had expressed interest in funding the growth of the men's program, he'd seemed a gift from fate. Since then, Vince had demonstrated mood swings and a knack for throwing everyone off balance, but his donation remained the hospital's best chance of acquiring the building and boosting the men's fertility program to the next level.

Lucky entered the hospital via the staff door. Instantly, his senses registered tempting aromas from the cafeteria. Also nearby, the chatter of childish voices drifted from the day care center, to which he presumed Zora would soon be entrusting her babies.

As he shoved open the door to the stairs—Lucky seized any chance at exercise—he wondered how long he could go without nagging her. *Somebody* had to advocate for those kids, who deserved their father's financial support even if he was incapable of acting like a real dad.

What about this Zady character? If she was a family member, Zora could sure use the help.

On the fifth floor, Lucky passed the executive offices and entered a smaller suite. The receptionist had apparently gone to lunch, and an inner door stood ajar. The placard read, Edmond Everhart, Family Law Consultant.

Lucky listened in case a client remained inside. Hearing no one, he rapped on the frame.

"Come in." From behind the desk, Edmond rose to greet

him. In his early thirties, like Lucky, and also about five-ten, the guy was impeccably dressed in a suit and tie. Only his rumpled brown hair revealed that he'd had a busy morning. All the same, there was nothing glib or calculating about him.

After shaking hands and taking a seat, Lucky went straight to the point. "I understand Vince Adams was souring on Safe Harbor until he talked to you. You spoke with him in public, so I presume client confidentiality doesn't apply."

"That's true." Leaning back, the attorney removed his glasses, plucked a microfiber cloth from the drawer and polished the lenses.

"I'm curious how you won him over, because—" Lucky couldn't go into detail, since it involved Vince's treatment "—just in case he changes his mind again. What upset him in the first place?"

"He felt disrespected because the whole hospital is aware that he has fertility issues," Edmond said.

"A fact that he's publicized with his own…statements." Lucky had nearly said *big mouth*.

"Be that as it may, he believed people looked down on him because he can't father children."

"How'd you reassure him?"

"I shared a few personal details that put us on a par." After a hesitation, Edmond continued, "I explained that I'd had a vasectomy and later regretted it." His wife, Melissa, was carrying embryos donated by another couple. "I also asked his advice as a stepfather about parenting my niece while her mom's in prison. I'm not sure why, but the conversation eased his mind."

"My guess is that he felt you respected him," Lucky mused. "Did he bring up anything else?"

Edmond reflected. "Yes. He's frustrated with his wife's refusal to consider in vitro. She wasn't present, so I have no idea how she views the matter."

Lucky recalled Zora's comments. "And he rejects hiring a surrogate?" The hospital maintained a roster of screened candidates.

"That's right."

Wheels spun in Lucky's head. "If we persuaded Mrs. Adams to change her mind, that ought to solve the problem."

"It might," Edmond said. "But is it wise to try to manipulate a woman into having a child she might not want?"

"I believe she's worried more about the medical risk than about having another child." At a previous office visit, a successfully treated patient had arrived to show Cole his newborn son. In the waiting room, Portia Adams had reached out to touch the baby's cheek and studied the child wistfully. Catching Lucky's eye, she'd murmured something about missing those days now that her girls were growing up.

"Perhaps there's a compromise position that might satisfy them both," Edmond said. "What if his wife provided the eggs but didn't carry the pregnancy?"

Lucky hadn't thought about separating the two aspects of in vitro. "It's worth a try."

"Good," Edmond said. "Any other questions?"

"Yes, although it's unrelated." While Lucky had promised not to pressure Zora, he hadn't promised not to encourage others to do so. "Zora hasn't broken the news to her ex about the twins. You're her attorney. How about pointing out that the man has legal obligations?"

The attorney laced his fingers atop the desk. "I assure you, I already have."

"You may have to get in her face, so she can't brush you off."

Edmond tilted his head. "May I share something with you that I've discovered about relationships?"

"Sure." Lucky admired how much Edmond had grown and changed while reconciling with Melissa. "Lay it on me."

"It's important to respect her choices," Edmond said.

"Even if you disagree with them?"

"Especially if you disagree with them." Thoughtfully, the lawyer added, "And especially when she's the person who has to deal with the consequences."

"But Zora keeps repeating the same boneheaded mistakes," Lucky protested.

"I suspect she understands her ex-husband better than either of us," Edmond said. "Legally, she'll have to inform him about the babies once they're born, but until then, she might have reason to be cautious."

Lucky only knew Andrew by reputation. "I suppose it's hard to predict how a guy will react to that kind of news."

"Exactly."

The circumstances might not be perfect, but this was a situation of Andrew's own making. Any decent guy would accept responsibility. However, the man had proven repeatedly that he didn't care about honor *or* decency. "Thanks for the words of wisdom."

"You're welcome."

"Oh, one more thing," Lucky said as they both rose. "Does Zora have a sister named Zady?"

"I believe that's her twin," Edmond said.

"Thanks." A twin. Damn! By applying for the job, Zady had put Lucky in a delicate position. He felt as if he ought to alert Zora, but her sister's application was confidential.

He set off for the cafeteria, anxious to arrive before Zora finished eating so he could get her opinion about his discussion with Edmond. As for her mysterious twin, he'd better leave that hot potato alone.

BEING AROUND PERFECT people filled Zora with a sense of inadequacy. It was balanced by a fervent desire to figure out how they did it.

Take her obstetrician. Six feet tall with dramatic red

hair and green eyes, Paige Brennan was a doctor, mother to an eighteen-month-old daughter and wife of the head of a detective agency. Everyone admired and adored her, including her nurse, Keely, who could barely stand most people.

Busy as she was, Dr. Brennan had fit in Zora's exam during her lunch break. The woman was a step from sainthood.

As she sat on the examining table, Zora doubted she could ever develop such an air of confidence. As for inspiring others, she'd settle for earning their good-natured tolerance.

"Surely you have *some* questions," the doctor said after listening to the babies' heartbeats and reviewing Zora's weight gain and test results. They were fine considering her stage of pregnancy. "You never mention any problems."

"Am I supposed to?" Zora had been raised to consider complaining a sign of weakness.

"Frankly, yes." The tall woman draped her frame over a stool. "At thirty-two weeks with a multiple pregnancy, you must be having trouble sleeping, and your ankles are swollen. As I've suggested before, you should be on bed rest."

"I can't afford it," Zora said. "I don't have a husband to wait on me."

"What about the rest of your family?" the doctor asked.

"My mom and stepfather live in Oregon." She'd rather not have either of them around. And there was no sense bringing up her twin, perfect Zady with her ideal husband and kids, whom their mother never failed to mention when she talked with Zora.

The doctor's forehead creased. "Is your mom flying down for the birth?"

"Not if I have anything to say about it." Her mother would expect to be catered to, regardless of the circumstances. She'd be no help with a baby. At home, Mom waited on Zora's surly, demanding stepfather, but her attitude toward her daughters—toward Zora, at least—was just the opposite.

Dr. Brennan regarded her with concern. "Have you chosen a labor partner?" At every visit, she'd recommended Zora sign up for a birthing class.

"I won't need one for a C-section." Although twins didn't always have to be delivered surgically, Zora preferred to play it safe.

"If that's what you want, okay." The physician nodded. "But remember that what we call bed rest doesn't necessarily require staying in bed. You can relax at home and perform routine tasks as you feel capable."

"I feel capable of working." To forestall further objections, Zora added, "And providing ultrasounds doesn't harm the babies. It's not like X-rays or mammograms."

"But it does require standing on your feet all day. And for safety's sake, you should stop driving." Paige raised her eyebrows commandingly.

Zora *was* having trouble reaching the pedals in her car. "I could ride to work with my housemates." Rod, whose car frequently broke down, cadged rides from others, so why shouldn't she?

Keely chose that moment to step in from the hall. "I can drive her."

"Excuse me?" Paige blinked at the unexpected comment.

"If I rent a room in their house, Zora can ride with me." The nurse mustered a faint smile.

"I thought you had a roommate," Zora said.

"So did I. Can we talk at lunch?"

"Sure."

The obstetrician cleared her throat. "Keely, would you provide Zora with an after-visit summary and schedule an appointment for her in two weeks?"

"Yes, Doctor."

The doctor typed a note into the computer. "Zora, call

me if you have any problems, such as spotting or contractions, even if they don't hurt. Okay?"

"Will do." Zora accepted the nurse's assistance in rising from the table.

Once she was dressed, she tucked the printed summary into her purse and walked to the elevator with Keely. With her neck thrust forward, the woman's aggressive stance reinforced the impression of her as a difficult personality. Zora hoped she hadn't erred by suggesting Keely move in with them.

"What's the situation with your roommate?" she asked as they descended. The office was only one flight up, but in Zora's condition, that might as well be ten stories.

"She's in Iowa taking care of her mother," Keely said. "She only planned to stay a week but that's changed. Last night she emailed and asked me to ship all her stuff to her."

"That was short notice. Your rent must be due next week." It was the first of the month.

"That's right. I'm glad you mentioned the vacancy."

"Everything's subject to Karen's approval," Zora warned.

"I'll stop by her office later."

It sounded like a done deal. At least Keely would be an improvement on Laird.

In the cafeteria, the blend of voices and aromas filled Zora with eagerness to share this new development with Lucky. Where was he? Her gaze swept past the food serving bays and across the crowded room.

She spotted him sharing a table with a thin and most unwelcome companion: Laird. The psychologist was talking a mile a minute, oblivious to Lucky's irritated expression.

Zora would rather not discuss Keely in front of the competition. "Hold on," she said, turning.

Too late. Keely was stomping right over to the table. Judging by the set of her shoulders, she didn't plan to be subtle, either.

Chapter Five

Lucky had often heard the flow of gossip referred to as a grapevine, but in a hospital, a more appropriate comparison would be the circulatory system, with its arteries and veins. And its heart, the pump through which all rumors flowed, was the cafeteria.

As a rule, he enjoyed the hum of conversations, among which his ears caught intriguing snatches of news— about hirings and firings, love affairs and broken hearts. Once in a while the drama expanded to include the doctors.

Until today, however, Lucky hadn't understood the embarrassment of landing in the middle of a scene that drew all eyes. It started when Keely announced, without preamble, "I lost my roommate. I've decided to move into your house!"

People peered toward them. The story of Karen's home, its assorted occupants and the resulting pregnancies and marriages had already set many a tongue wagging.

Laird choked, although Lucky couldn't figure out on what. The psychologist hadn't stopped yammering long enough to eat anything. Instead, he'd plopped his butt into a chair at Lucky's table and begun citing his plans for throwing parties.

He'd also proclaimed that his huge TV screen would transform their outdated living room into game central.

Not that Lucky would mind, but the guy apparently didn't consider it necessary to solicit *Karen's* opinion.

"Like hell you're moving in!" Laird finally blurted in a voice that rose to a squeal. "Whatever gave you that idea?"

"I cleared it with Zora." Keely indicated that red-haired person, who gazed warily from the hot food line before ducking out of sight.

Lucky nearly bellowed, "Get over here!" but more heads were swiveling. Not his doctor, mercifully. Through the glass doors, he spotted Dr. Rattigan out of earshot on the patio.

"It's a party house!" Laird, his usually pale face reddening with anger, didn't appear to care who heard him roar. "You're the last person in Safe Harbor anyone would invite to a party."

Silence fell save for the clink of tableware and glasses. The chatter of a man talking on a cell phone sounded abnormally loud, and then that too ceased.

"Let's skip the insults, shall we?" Lucky deliberately employed a soft tone in the hope the others would follow suit.

The effort fell flat. "Oh, really?" Keely boomed. "I was invited to the baby shower, in case you forgot. As for you, Laird, you can take your grabby hands and go live in a brothel."

Lucky wouldn't show cowardice by retreating from the scene. But he could remove himself from the line of fire on the pretext of assisting the pregnant lady.

"Excuse me." Springing up, he narrowly restrained the temptation to break into a run.

Behind him, Laird snarled something about Keely being jealous because nobody made passes at her. Whatever the nurse responded, Lucky shut it out.

"Let me help with that," he told Zora, who had set down her tray as she paid for her lunch. He seized the tray without waiting for permission.

She stepped away from the register. "People are staring."

"Can you blame them?" Lucky halted as a tableful of volunteers arose, blocking their path. Grateful for the delay, he smiled encouragingly at an elderly lady, a gift shop regular who creaked to her feet at glacial speed. To Zora, he asked, "How'd you hook up with Keely?"

"She glommed on to me at Dr. Brennan's office," she explained.

"You had to see the doctor? You aren't having problems, are you?"

"Routine checkup."

"You sure?" He searched her face for signs of pain. She had a bad habit of toughing things out, but she looked well enough today.

What a sweet face, he thought, with a full mouth and a youthful sprinkling of freckles. Standing this close to Zora was having a weird effect on him. In light of their new pact, he wasn't sure how to respond to her. It had been easier when he could drop a comment about Andrew into any conversation and receive a predictably angry retort.

"Did you promise Keely she could move in?" That ought to stir a response.

"Yes, but I warned her Karen has the final say." Biting her lip, Zora peered toward Keely and Laird, who were continuing to insult each other. They'd lowered their voices a notch, but at this stage it only meant other diners leaned forward in their seats to hear them. One orderly went so far as to cup his hands around his ears. "She'd be a zillion percent better than Laird," Zora said.

"For once—twice, actually—we agree on something. Let's not make it a habit."

"Certainly not," Zora replied. "Life would get boring."

"I'm sure we'll find plenty to squabble about." Lucky dodged away as the elderly volunteer snapped her cane to the floor inches from his foot. "Hey!"

She ambled out, not hearing him. Another volunteer responded with a quiet, "Sorry."

"Excellent reaction time," Zora observed.

"Thanks."

They resumed their journey toward the table, where Laird and Keely stood with arms folded, as if whoever was victorious in their staring contest would win the privilege of moving into the house. Around them, conversations slowly resumed.

"Isn't Keely eating lunch?" Lucky murmured. "She didn't stop to pick up anything."

"Look on the bright side," Zora said. "They can't have a food fight."

"I'd enjoy a food fight," he teased.

"Of course you would."

"I didn't say I'd participate." He lowered her tray onto the table beside his. "Guys, how about easing off?"

"Not till we settle this," Keely said.

"We can't do that without…" He broke off at the approach of their landlady, who projected authority despite being no taller than Zora. Maybe it was this month's black hair or the distinctive long skirts she favored, but more likely it was the quelling expression she wore. "Hey, Karen," he ventured.

Her frosty gaze swept the four of them. "Have a seat, everyone, and stop creating a spectacle."

They obeyed. "Now, what is this about?" Raising a hand to stop a barrage of words, Karen said, "Starting with Keely."

As the nurse explained about her roommate departing on short notice, Lucky watched Zora tuck into her food and thought about her twin. How could there be a carbon copy of her anywhere in the world? Surely no one had the same fiery temperament, or the same gift for frustrating the hell out of him while appealing to his masculine instincts. And why was Zady seeking to work near her sister, when the two appeared to be estranged?

Still, twins were supposed to have a special bond, in contrast to Lucky and his older brother. He didn't even know where Matthew lived now or whether he was still serving in the navy, and he didn't care.

Best friends during their teens, they hadn't spoken in sixteen years. Their last fight, after their parents' deaths, had been too bitter for either of them to forgive. Lucky deeply regretted his mistakes, but that didn't give his brother the right to make vicious, unfair accusations and repeat them to other family members. As a result, Lucky had distanced himself not only from Matthew but also from his aunts, uncles and cousins.

When Keely paused for breath, Laird jumped in. He insisted he had a prior claim and that the household needed him to liven things up.

"I wasn't aware we were dull," Karen snapped. "Frankly, after the behavior I just witnessed, I'd drop you both from consideration, but for financial reasons, I need someone to move in next weekend."

Laird lifted his chin. "Considering my position as staff psychologist, I outrank this woman."

Didn't the jerk realize he'd insulted Lucky, who was an RN on a par with Keely? And Karen herself held the middle-level post of financial counselor.

"This isn't a promotional position," she said. "No offense, Laird, but I think having a nurse across the hall from a pregnant woman would be the most sensible choice. However, I won't approve anyone without the consent of my other renters. Lucky? Zora?"

Nobody wished to become Laird's enemy. Nevertheless, Lucky tilted his head toward Keely, as did Zora. Turning, Karen pinpointed Rod. The anesthesiologist, who was sitting with his nephew and several other doctors, mouthed, "Kee-lee."

If Lucky imagined they'd fallen below everyone else's radar, a rustle of movement proved otherwise as people shifted to observe Rod, then moved their attention back to his table.

"I'm sorry," Karen told the psychologist. "The group agrees with my rationale."

Laird scrambled to his feet. "I hope you'll keep me in mind if there's another opening. Keely might not fit in as well as you assume."

"You're the one who doesn't fit in," the nurse sneered.

"You'll regret this." Noticing everyone's reaction to this threat, Laird added, "I mean, it wouldn't surprise me if they threw you out in a few months."

He stalked off, leaving his dirty dishes. Nostrils flaring, Keely watched him go before excusing herself to buy food.

"Alone at last," Lucky teased after Karen, too, departed.

Zora swallowed a mouthful of milk and wasted no time changing the subject. "Did you talk to Edmond?"

He sketched what he'd learned about Vince and Portia Adams. "My plan is to encourage her to donate eggs and him to hire a gestational surrogate."

"Splitting the difference? Excellent," Zora said. "I suspect you're right about Portia's maternal instincts. During Tiffany's last visit, she mentioned that her mom's developed a fascination with her friends' babies."

"Any suggestions how to nudge her further in that direction?"

"Talk to Rod," she advised.

First she'd recommended he consult Edmond, now Rod. "Why?"

"He used to be married to Portia. If anyone can comprehend how her mind works, it's him." Having polished off her entrée, Zora tackled her custard.

He should have thought of that, Lucky mused. But a marriage that had ended bitterly half a dozen years ago hardly qualified the anesthesiologist as an expert. "You're a mom, or soon will be. Put me into her perspective about this pregnancy business."

"She's a fashion plate who I'm sure injects stuff into her wrinkles and suctions her flab," Zora said. "It's partly ego but I also think she feels she has to compete for her husband's affection. How's she going to fend off gold diggers ten years younger when she has a big round pregnant body?"

"But donating eggs might be okay?"

"Better, although those hormone shots and the mood swings aren't fun," Zora said.

Lucky sighed. "Well, thanks for bouncing ideas around with me."

"Glad to do it." Abruptly, Zora set down her fork. "Something just hit me."

If it would help bring the Adamses together, he was eager to hear it. "Yes?"

"I—" She broke off as a ringtone sounded and she took out her phone. "This is Zora."

Lucky could happily have smashed the device for interrupting them. "Don't lose that thought!"

Frowning, Zora answered. "Yes? Now? Okay. I'll be right there." She clicked off. "It's radiology."

How frustrating. "Before you go, tell me what occurred to you."

"No time. We can discuss it tonight." Hands on the table, Zora hoisted herself upright. "Will you dispose of my dishes? I'd hate to be a slob like Laird."

"Of course," he said. "But—"

"It's a patient of Dr. Tartikoff's," she explained. "The tech went home sick, and he's waiting with her."

Nobody wished to cross the imperious head of the fertility program. "I understand."

"Thanks, Lucky," she said. "I can always count on you."

It was on the tip of his tongue to note that she ought to be able to rely on the father of her children, but he'd promised to lay off that subject. And Lucky found it rather gratifying that he and no one else was the person she counted on.

TALKING TO LUCKY was more fun now that he no longer poked at her sore spot, Zora reflected as she lumbered along the sidewalk to the medical office building. And even though she hadn't planned it, she'd rather enjoyed needling him by withholding information.

On the third floor, she entered Dr. T's medical suite and headed for the room set up for the ultrasound. Nurse Ned Norwalk, a surfer type with a deep tan, appeared around a corner. "You?" he demanded.

"Me, what?" Zora asked. Although she and Ned moved in different circles, she'd never had any problems with him.

"There wasn't any other tech available?" He obviously didn't expect an answer. "Never mind. Fair warning—Dr. T hasn't eaten lunch."

Great—he'd be crankier than ever. "I'll tiptoe around. Where's the patient's chart?"

"The doctor has it. The patient has a mass on her right ovary. You'll be doing a transvaginal ultrasound."

"Okay." Sonograms to examine ovarian cysts—fluid-filled pockets in or on the surface of an ovary—as well as other growths were commonplace. While most cysts vanished on their own, some caused pain, and there was the scary possibility that an ovarian growth could be cancerous. The best view of the ovaries was obtained by inserting a probe into the patient's vagina. "Is she pregnant?"

"No. But—you're sure there wasn't anyone else available?"

"If you doubt me, call radiology."

"Never mind."

Zora had often assisted Dr. T's patients. She didn't understand why Ned was making a big deal of this, but she didn't intend to question him and keep the great physician waiting.

Ned opened the door and retreated. Near the small ultrasound machine paced a scowling Dr. Owen Tartikoff. Even his russet hair seemed to be sizzling with impatience. "Finally," he growled.

"Sorry for the delay. The scheduled tech went home sick." Zora's gaze shifted to the dark-haired woman lying on the examining table, her lower half covered with a paper sheet.

When almond-shaped brown eyes met hers with a jolt, Zora struggled to catch her breath. The patient was Lin Lee Raditch, Andrew's third wife.

Although they'd never been introduced, she'd seen the woman with him around town, and judging by the other woman's reaction, Lin recognized Zora, as well. That explained Ned's attitude. Either the scheduler hadn't noticed that they shared a last name, or had no other options.

"Is there a problem?" The doctor's cross tone slapped at her. He didn't seem aware of their connection.

Zora darted a glance at Lin. The patient had the right to object to an inappropriate care provider. And for the sake of her own emotional state, Zora wasn't sure she ought to go through with this.

Lin's lips pressed tightly. Was she reluctant to offend the celebrated doctor? Then Zora noticed tears glittering in the patient's eyes. *She's frightened.*

In that instant, Lin transformed from the jezebel for whom Andrew had abandoned Zora into a scared woman who might face a terrifying diagnosis.

"This won't hurt," she assured the patient, and went to work.

Chapter Six

"These appear to be fluid-filled cysts," Dr. Tartikoff told the patient as Zora finished her scan. "However, before recommending a treatment plan, I'll have the radiologist review the images."

"It isn't cancer?" Lin's body had gone nearly rigid, although Zora had encouraged her to relax during the procedure.

"I doubt it." The obstetrician continued studying the screen. "If these were solid, or partially solid, I'd be more concerned."

The patient swallowed, evidently still worried. "Will you have to remove my ovaries?"

"It may be possible to perform a cystectomy, excising only the largest cyst." Dr. T patted Lin's shoulder reassuringly. "Or we might remove one ovary, leaving the other in place."

"I can still have children?" Lin's slightly accented voice trembled.

"Yes, but first let's deal with the discomfort you've been suffering."

"Thank you, Doctor." She regarded him gratefully.

How ironic, Zora thought, that Andrew's wife was concerned about being able to bear his children, while Zora herself stood there with his babies thumping inside her.

Nevertheless, her heart went out to the anxious young woman.

Did life have to be so complicated? It would be easier if Zora could simply blame Andrew's faithlessness on his new wife. Instead, she related to Lin's pain. Carrying twins was hard, but being unable to bear children would be worse.

"The radiologist's report should reach me within a few days. I'll review it immediately," Dr. T advised. "Please set up an appointment for next week. Your husband should accompany you."

Lin's smile vanished. "He travels and is very busy."

"You're his wife. There's nothing more important than your health." In his intensity, Zora heard the conviction of a man devoted to his wife and children. "Would you like me to explain the situation to him?"

"No, no, Doctor, that isn't necessary." Lin sounded anxious.

"You're sure?"

When she again declined, Dr. T excused himself and left.

"I'll be out of here in a minute so you can dress," Zora said. She shifted the equipment cart away from the examining table.

Lin touched her arm. "Thank you for being gentle."

Astonished, Zora wondered what the woman had expected. "You're welcome."

"I am wondering…" She indicated Zora's expanded midsection.

Was she asking about the father? Zora pretended not to pick up the hint. "Twins," she said. "Due in late November."

"You are fortunate to be fertile." The patient sat up. "I am desperate for children to bind my husband to me and prove my family is wrong."

"Wrong about what?" Zora asked.

"They believe I married a man who will treat me badly."
She sniffled. "And they're angry that I moved to another
country after they sacrificed to send me to college. My
mother will not talk to me on the phone."

On the verge of inquiring why Lin was sharing this with
her of all people, Zora realized how isolated the woman
was. "That must be difficult." She handed over a tissue.

Lin wiped her eyes. "Pardon me, but also, I wonder
why you are pregnant when you did not want children."

A weird sense of déjà vu swept over Zora. During her
marriage, Andrew had claimed his first wife had refused
to have kids. Only later had she learned that the opposite
was true: Stacy had longed for children but delayed pregnancy at Andrew's request.

Same lies, same manipulations. Pain knifed inside Zora.
Lucky's right. I must be the most gullible person on earth.

"What is wrong?" Gathering the paper covering her,
Lin eased off the table. "The babies are hurting you?"

This show of compassion undid her. Suddenly Zora
couldn't hold her secret inside for another instant. "Andrew lied to you. These are his children, except he doesn't
know that yet."

Lin stood frozen with her bare feet on the linoleum.
"That is impossible. He had a vasectomy. You insisted
on it."

"No, I didn't. When…?" Zora gave a start at a tap on
the door.

Ned Norwalk entered, holding a sheet of paper. "How's
everything in here?" The nurse halted at the sight of them
obviously engaged in a discussion. "Are you okay, Mrs.
Raditch?"

"I'm fine," both women said.

"The current Mrs. Raditch."

They glared at him.

He blinked, registering the unexpected collusion, and,

to his credit, decided to respect their privacy. "I'll be at the nurses' station if anyone wants me."

After Ned beat a strategic retreat, Zora refocused on her companion. "If Andrew had a vasectomy, it wasn't at my request. And these *are* his children."

"You are wrong," Lin insisted. "He showed me the scar."

Zora preferred not to think about the location of that scar or the intimate circumstances under which he'd displayed it. "When was that?"

The other woman, a few inches shorter than her, considered briefly before saying, "Eight months ago, while we were engaged. Before you became pregnant, if you are in the seventh month."

Could he have faked the scar? Then a better explanation occurred to Zora.

"After a vasectomy, a man's sperm count doesn't immediately drop to zero. It can take a month or more before the sperm is completely gone." She absorbed a lot of medical information in her work. "We were still married—barely. He must have been fertile, because I haven't slept with anyone else."

Lin steadied herself on the edge of the examining table. "These babies, they really are his?"

"I'm afraid so. It all makes more sense now. No wonder he didn't insist on contraception—he'd had a vasectomy." Zora had assumed that, at some level, Andrew had wished to father a baby with her. Instead, he'd believed he was safe.

Lin hugged herself and shivered. "You will take away my husband."

That was precisely what Zora had fantasized. Now, witnessing the other woman's distress, she faced the fact that Andrew had coldheartedly plucked Lin from her family and country, then lied to her and manipulated her. He'd also played on Zora's love for him, using and discarding her yet again. Why? For ego's sake?

The man had no heart and could never be trusted. Zora was truly alone in this pregnancy. Except for Lucky. And her other friends, of course.

To her astonishment, the primary emotion pumping through her was relief. She didn't have to pretend any more. She could tell the truth, to herself most of all.

"I don't want him back," Zora said.

The dark-haired woman studied her in confusion. "But you carry his babies."

The man isn't capable of loving anyone except himself. A burden lifted from her shoulders, filling her with unaccustomed lightness despite the weight in her womb. "You can keep him with my blessing."

A couple of quick steps and Lin flung her arms around Zora. "You are my sister in spirit. I shall try to be strong like you."

Zora hesitated only a second before returning the hug. When she and Andrew broke up, she'd been utterly friendless. That experience intensified her empathy with this woman whose world was collapsing. "What will you do?"

Lin breathed deeply before replying, "I will think hard."

"If you need a divorce attorney, I recommend Edmond Everhart," Zora said. "He's a consultant on staff at the hospital."

"That is good advice," Lin said.

"Best of luck."

As Zora exited, she ignored a questioning look from Ned in the hall. Struggling to sort through what she'd learned, she wished she didn't have to endure Lucky's comments when he heard about this encounter.

And yet, she felt liberated. "Sorry, babies," Zora whispered. "We're all better off without your dad."

Then fear quivered through her. How could she raise

these kids without a father? Her own might have been flawed, but she'd always sensed that he loved her and Zady.

Unlike her dad, Andrew lacked the capacity to care about others. Zora had to accept that and move on, no matter how badly it hurt.

She hoped she wouldn't have to put up with any I-told-you-so taunts tonight from Lucky, who would no doubt hear about this entire scene via the gossip mill. With her heart aching and her mood unsettled, she was in no mood to tolerate his sniping.

WITH EVERYONE EAGER to chat about Keely's pending arrival, Lucky and his three housemates gathered at the dining room table earlier than usual on Monday night. While they ate, they relived the scene in the cafeteria and speculated about Laird's not-so-veiled threat.

Would he try to intimidate Keely to keep her from joining them? Did he honestly believe they'd accept him if he did?

Karen related that Keely had paid a deposit and arranged to move in Saturday afternoon. Her only question had been whether the nearness to the estuary caused illness among the residents. Karen had assured her that, despite the smell, they all stayed remarkably healthy.

Questions and comments flew, but the usually talkative Zora didn't join in, Lucky noted. Instead, she downed her soup and salad while avoiding his gaze. Was she annoyed at him?

Perhaps she'd found out about her twin applying for a job. After reviewing the remaining résumés, he'd confirmed that Zady's qualifications merited a spot among the top half dozen contenders and had scheduled her for an interview next week, when the new urologist would be visiting. But if that was the problem, why wasn't Zora interrogating him?

During a lull in the conversation, she slanted a glare

at him. He'd done nothing to deserve that, Lucky was almost certain. "What?" he demanded.

"What do you mean, what?"

"I mean, why are you scowling at me? I haven't done anything." *Recently.*

"You will," she muttered.

"Suit yourself." Lucky let the subject drop. If he'd offended Zora, it was her responsibility to be frank about it.

Rod and Karen finished eating and carried their dishes into the kitchen. As Zora started to rise, Lucky recalled her hasty departure from lunch and the idea she'd mentioned. "Hold on a sec."

She grimaced. "We might as well get this over with."

"Get what over with?"

Still not meeting his gaze, she said, "I refuse to make it easier for you."

He was growing more confused by the minute. She'd been friendly at lunch, and Lucky had been too busy during the afternoon to ruffle anyone's feathers. To compensate for his absence at the convention, Dr. Rattigan had squeezed in so many patients that Lucky had skipped his coffee break and stayed at the office late.

"Is this about your—" He nearly said *sister*, but caught himself. Besides, there was another thing he'd been waiting to discuss. "Idea about the Adamses?" he finished.

"What idea about the Adamses?"

"In the cafeteria, you said something hit you, and then you took off to see a patient," Lucky reminded her.

"Did I?" Zora rested her chin in her palm. Pregnancy had darkened her cute freckles and rounded her cheeks. Her hair had thickened and taken on a shine, as well.

"Please don't tell me you forgot the idea."

She frowned so hard that Lucky feared she'd get a headache. Then she brightened. "I remember!"

"Shoot."

"Portia has mixed feelings about pregnancy because

she fears it will turn Vince away from her, but she might change her mind if she realizes it could save her marriage," Zora said.

"Why is she so afraid of losing him?" Lucky countered. "In a divorce, she could take her husband to the cleaners."

"There's always the possibility that she loves the guy. Besides, from what I've read, Vince's previous two wives didn't fare very well," she replied.

Lucky recalled news reports about the man's insistence on prenuptial agreements. Nevertheless, the women had been left financially comfortable by ordinary standards. "A few million apiece might not be much compared to his billions, but it ain't too shabby."

"It's not only the money." Rod joined the conversation from the kitchen entrance. "Portia loves having a ringside seat at New York Fashion Week, being invited to A-list parties and hobnobbing with celebrities. A couple of million dollars doesn't do that. Being married to Vince Adams does."

Lucky supposed Rod knew her better than any of them. "Wouldn't having a baby interfere with all that partying?"

"Not when you can afford live-in nannies," he growled.

"You can be a devoted mom and still hire a nanny," Zora said. "Don't forget, she has lots of free time during the day, since she doesn't work."

"Portia will do whatever she believes is in her best interest, and to hell with anyone else," Rod snarled, and ducked out of sight.

While Lucky had a less jaundiced view of Mrs. Adams than Rod, he did agree that she'd fight to save her marriage. "Interesting point," he told Zora. "It's worth bearing in mind."

Silence descended, aside from random noises in the kitchen. Zora poked at the remaining bits of lettuce on her salad plate. "Stop torturing me."

He might as well take the bull by the horns, Lucky decided. "Is this about your sister?"

"My sister?" Her blank expression indicated he'd missed the mark.

He had to cover his mistake, fast. "I heard you have a twin sister."

"From who?"

He couldn't cite the job application and he'd rather avoid implicating Edmond, who'd merely confirmed what Lucky had already stumbled across. "Informed sources."

"She's none of your business," Zora snapped. "We aren't in touch. Stop changing the subject."

Rod stuck his head through the door again. "Oh, seriously, Lucky, quit acting coy. Everyone's dying to find out what happened between the two Mrs. Raditches."

That was what had gone down today? And he hadn't heard a word.

Lucky threw up his hands. "I skip my coffee break for one afternoon and miss the gossip of the century. You went mano a mano with the new Mrs. Raditch?"

"She's a patient. I can't discuss…" To his dismay, Zora's face crumpled, and tears rolled down her cheeks.

Lucky scooted over and put his arms around her, enjoying the warmth of her pregnancy-enhanced body. "You discovered she's no more a demon than you are, and Andrew's an even bigger rat than you realized. Am I close?"

"I feel bad for her." Zora scrubbed her cheek with the back of her hand. "Her family rejected her when she married him. She's alone in a foreign country. And he lied about me, like he lied about Stacy. As if we're interchangeable."

To Lucky, there was nothing interchangeable about Zora and any other woman on the planet, including her twin. That was irrelevant, however. "You're crying for her sake?"

"And because what I learned means he'll never love

these babies. Before today, I believed that deep down, he wanted them." Her gray eyes darkened with sorrow. "Ever since I've been steeling myself for you to say, *I told you so*. Go ahead and get it over with."

Cradling her against him, Lucky said, "Okay. I told you so."

A painful whack in the ankle sent him jolting backward, nearly overturning his chair. "Ow! How'd you do that from this angle?" Releasing her, he rubbed the spot where she'd kicked him.

"Public opinion agrees that you deserved it," noted Rod, who'd resumed snooping from the doorway.

"Beat it," Zora ordered him.

"Me?" Rod feigned innocence.

"This is between me and this pain in the neck," she retorted.

"Pain in the ankle," Lucky corrected.

From behind Rod, a feminine hand gripped his shirt collar and tugged him out of sight. Lucky wafted a mental thanks in Karen's direction.

"If my shin is black-and-blue tomorrow, I'll sue for assault." He moved to a chair at a safer distance.

"Felled by a pregnant midget?" Zora wisecracked. "What a wimp."

Footsteps moved through the den and around to the front. The stairs creaked as their housemates ascended, leaving them in privacy.

Once Lucky heard Karen's door close upstairs, he felt safe to ask, "What's your next move?"

Zora stretched her legs under the table. "I talked to Edmond. He says Andrew has to pay half of the uninsured costs for my pregnancy and half the child-care expenses."

"You'll let the attorney deal with him?" That seemed wise.

Zora nodded. "I'm still not sure how I'd react to Andrew in the flesh."

"More importantly, how would he react to *you*?" Lucky's hands formed fists at the idea of the man bullying Zora.

"I hate being weak." She dabbed her eyes with her napkin.

"There's nothing weak about using good judgment," he said. "You don't have to prove how tough you are."

"That's not what I mean." She indicated her enlarged abdomen. "When I'm alone with Andrew, he slips past my defenses. Here's the living proof."

"You can seize control if you're determined." Surely she could resist the man after everything he'd put her through. "Zora, you're strength personified with everyone else."

"Am I?" She gazed into space. "My dad used to swing between being a jerk and being the most loving father in the world. No matter how hard I resolved to stay angry, I couldn't."

"Did he drink?" In Lucky's observation, alcoholism was often associated with that sort of behavior.

"Yes, sometimes." Zora inhaled deeply. "I used to long for a family I could rely on, where people were actually happy. That's still my dream, I guess."

It was Lucky's, too, he reflected with a lump in his throat. Money had been tight for his family when he'd been young, and his parents had struggled to keep their store profitable. There'd always been love, but there'd been stress and long work hours, too.

While nothing could excuse the way Lucky had let them down, the pressure to help support the family had been difficult for him to handle as an immature teen. Before he risked establishing a family of his own, he'd make sure their finances were on a secure footing and find a wife who shared his values. Those included careful planning, postponing having kids and communicating honestly.

"What happened to your dad?" Lucky knew Zora's mom was a widow, but had never heard any details.

"When I was twenty-two, they had a big fight and he moved out." She paused, and then the words spilled out. "Mom claimed he'd cheated on her, which to me was such a betrayal of the whole family that I refused to speak to him. A few months later, he dropped dead of a heart attack. We never said goodbye."

"I'm sorry." What a burden of guilt that must place on her. "It wasn't your fault."

"If you love somebody, shouldn't you keep trying to rescue the relationship?"

"But past a certain point, you're only enabling him." Lucky eased farther away in case she tried kicking him again.

Instead, Zora lurched to her feet. "Well, I'm done enabling Andrew. Edmond can handle him from now on."

"I agree in principle." Reaching over, Lucky collected her dishes and piled them with his. "You can't avoid him forever, though."

"I can try." A pounding on the front door sent Zora's hand flying to her throat. "Oh, my gosh, you don't suppose that's him, do you?"

The thuds grew louder. "Stay there. I'll get it." After depositing the dishes in the kitchen, Lucky went to answer.

On the porch, hand raised for renewed hammering, stood a man of about thirty, a tailored suit jacket failing to disguise his pudgy gut. Blond hair, blue eyes, sneering expression. "Andrew Raditch?" Lucky guessed.

"Where is she?" The man stomped in. Had Lucky not dodged him, they'd have collided. "I insist on talking to my wife."

"Which wife would that be?" Finally, here was the man who'd created endless trouble—and, Lucky conceded, a measure of entertainment—over the past few months. Andrew was shorter than he'd imagined, and not nearly handsome enough to explain his appeal to women.

"Don't mess with me, mister." Feet planted in the entry, Andrew bellowed, "Zora, where the hell are you?"

How could this rude oaf be the son of Betsy Raditch? But then, he had alcohol on his breath.

From around the corner of the staircase, Zora regarded her ex-husband coolly. "What's your problem, Andrew?"

"What did you say to Lin?" the man demanded. "She admitted to my face that she talked to you."

As if that were a crime, Lucky thought.

"So?" Still half in the living room as if prepared to dodge away, Zora watched him guardedly.

"She packed a bag and walked out on me," Andrew said. "She was crying. Did you enjoy hurting her?"

"I'm not the one who hurt her." Zora remained admirably calm, in Lucky's opinion.

"You must have filled her head with lies!" Andrew smacked his hand against the wall.

"You accuse *me* of lying?" Zora stood her ground. "You should study the definition of truth. It seems to be an alien concept to you."

"Cut the crap." Andrew prowled toward her. "You call Lin right now and apologize."

"For what?"

"For whatever you…" As Zora stepped into full view, big belly and all, Andrew's jaw worked without producing another sound.

Lucky enjoyed the man's shock. Finally, Andrew had discovered he was going to be a father.

Chapter Seven

To Zora, Andrew seemed different tonight. Was it the extra
height of the ceiling that dwarfed him or the contrast between him and Lucky? Andrew's muscles from playing
high school football were running to fat—in contrast to
Lucky's well-toned build—and his once-thick blond hair
had begun receding at the temples.

As for his blustering manner, usually it yielded to calculated charm as soon as he saw that he'd intimidated her.
Tonight, though, with Lucky on hand and the memory of
the afternoon's anguished scene still raw, she remained
in control of her emotions. No intimidation, and hence no
charm to obscure his true reaction.

For a revealing moment, she watched Andrew's expression shift from disbelief to anger to disdain as he weighed
his response to her pregnancy. Before today, while Zora
had recognized the self-serving motives that rippled below
the man's slick surface, she'd soon been sucked under by
his charisma. Tonight, the curl of his lip and the flare of
his nostrils might have belonged to a stranger. A stranger
she disliked.

"Now I understand what you dropped on Lin." With a
wave of his arm, he indicated—and dismissed—her pregnancy. "You persuaded her it was mine, didn't you? I can't
imagine how you fooled her. She knows I had a vasectomy."

Behind him, Zora caught Lucky's startled blink. Funny how keenly she registered her housemate's responses, and how grateful she was for his protective stance.

"Your doctor did warn you that a vasectomy doesn't instantly render you sterile, I presume," she said.

"It takes a few weeks," her ex responded confidently. "I gave it a month."

He'd calculated the timing, or so he believed. "I have two words for you," Zora told Andrew. "Paternity test."

"You went out and slept with someone else," he sneered. "No doubt right after I signed the divorce papers."

"Did your doctor confirm that your sperm count had dropped to zero?" Lucky asked. In response to Andrew's who-the-hell-are-you? scowl, he added, "I work in a urologist's office. It takes ten to twenty ejaculations to completely clear the sperm."

Andrew paled. "The baby *can't* be mine."

"Babies, plural," Zora corrected.

"Beg pardon?"

"I'm carrying twins," she said. "And in California, a paternity test isn't necessary for you to owe child support. According to my attorney, if the parents are married, by law the husband is automatically the father. And we *were* still married that night."

At the memory, pain threatened her detachment. She'd dropped by Andrew's apartment to urge him to sign the divorce papers after weeks of him playing games. Instead, he'd sworn that he regretted cheating on her, declared that she was his true love and drawn her into his bed. A few nights later, while she nursed the hope that he planned to cast off his fiancée and stay with her, he'd dropped the signed divorce papers on her porch and fled.

"You waited, what, seven months to inform me?" His other tactics having failed, Andrew assumed the mantle of outrage. "Any man would doubt these children are his. I refuse to pay for what isn't mine."

"If you insist, I'll arrange for a test." Might as well seal the deal.

That didn't appear to be the answer he'd expected. "You'd risk your babies' safety by sticking a needle in there?"

"You're out-of-date, man," Lucky announced. "It doesn't take an invasive test to establish paternity anymore. They can extract the baby's DNA from the mother's blood with ninety-nine-point-nine percent accuracy."

Andrew grimaced. "Fine. Whatever."

Zora seized on his apparent consent. "The test's expensive and insurance won't cover it. Since you're insisting on it, you can pay."

He shifted on the balls of his feet. "Half."

She supposed arguing the point would be futile. Instead, she added, "Okay, but legally you also owe half of my other maternity-related expenses." Oh, drat, her voice was trembling. Did the man feel absolutely nothing after learning that he'd fathered two children-to-be? He hadn't asked their genders, or Zora's due date, or whether she'd selected names.

Names. She'd planned to let him choose those in the absurd belief that doing so would strengthen his connection to the twins. After tonight, though, Zora resolved that he'd have nothing to do with selecting the names if she could help it.

"Let's run that test before you start counting my money," Andrew snarled. He turned abruptly, sidestepped Lucky and stalked out of the house.

Zora struggled to catch her breath. Since learning of her pregnancy, she'd imagined this scene repeatedly, in a thousand variations. Anger and awe, apology and acceptance—she'd credited Andrew with those feelings. Well, he'd shown the anger. Aside from that, however, the only other thing he'd displayed was utter indifference to his own kids.

"High five or knuckle bump?" Grinning, Lucky raised his hand for her response.

She burst into sobs.

"What's wrong?" The man looked flummoxed. "Zora, you were magnificent. You stood up to every trick he threw at you. Didn't you hear me silently cheering you?"

She struggled for control. "How could I hear something silent?"

"It was written all over my face." His dark eyes glowed. "Tonight, I witnessed a miraculous transformation. Right here in our living room, you became a kick-ass superhero."

His praise felt wonderful. It also filled her with wariness, because she didn't deserve it. "I forced him to agree to a blood test, that's all."

"And hit him up for half your expenses."

"He hasn't paid yet."

"Zora!" Lucky gripped her gently under her arms. "I'd swing you around to celebrate, only I doubt the twins would appreciate it."

"You're right." The duo were squirming. At this stage, she'd read, their auditory functions had developed enough for them to hear the argument. How sad that on their first exposure to their father's voice, it had been filled with rage.

Already, the babies might be forming lifelong impressions of masculine and feminine behavior. She hoped that Lucky's gentler tones offset Andrew's harshness. "He didn't ask a single question about his children. Maybe it hasn't sunk in yet."

"And maybe he's a self-centered prick. If I accidentally fathered babies, I'd be determined to give them the best," Lucky assured her.

"You'd take care of their mother, wouldn't you? You'd never let her down." Zora caught her breath, unsure why his answer mattered so much.

"I certainly wouldn't whine and try to weasel out of

my obligations," Lucky responded. "But I'm doing everything in my power to avoid running that kind of risk. I won't be ready for a family till I pay off my education loans and save a down payment for a house. My kids deserve a happy childhood with two parents who're mature enough to provide them with stability."

Zora's spirits plummeted. During the confrontation with Andrew, she'd drawn strength from Lucky's nearness, from having a man care about her without making demands. Well, of course he didn't make demands, because he didn't want anything from her, as he'd just indicated. He wanted the perfect wife, the perfect family, and she was far from perfect.

Why can't he love me, messy life and all?

What was wrong with her? She didn't love Lucky. Or if she did, it was the casual, friendship kind of love. He wasn't her type. Too rough around the edges and too judgmental. Still, the way he'd stood by her these past months had been more than kind. It had been…fatherly. And maybe more.

He was still holding her. Still gazing at her fondly. "I wish my children had a father like you," Zora blurted.

Lucky stared down at her for a moment. Then he released her. "I appreciate the compliment, but these are Andrew's kids."

She was on the verge of pointing out the obvious, that her ex-husband didn't want them, when it struck her what Lucky really meant—that he couldn't or wouldn't be their father, either.

The discovery chilled Zora. How naive she'd been, to believe even for an instant that Lucky could fill the void in her heart. How utterly unrealistic. *Typical of me, I guess.*

"I'd better lie down," she said.

"I didn't mean to upset you," he responded. "I only meant…"

Zora waved away the explanation. "Don't bother. I'm a total idiot when it comes to relationships."

"Did I miss something?" Lucky asked.

How adorably clueless he was. "I'm tired. It's been a long day."

"It's only eight thirty."

Zora struggled to ignore his worried gaze. "That's late, for a pregnant woman." A pregnant woman whose last lingering illusions had been shattered.

Until tonight, her bond to Andrew—imaginary though it had been—had shielded her from any other man like a brick wall. Now, vulnerable and hurt, she seemed to be stumbling over a bunch of loose bricks. "Good night."

"If you're sure."

"I am." Zora hurried away, although she wasn't sure about anything. Okay, about the no-more-Andrew part, yes. But as for Lucky, somewhere along the line, love had mushroomed in the dark. What defense did she have against her best friend?

In her bedroom, she dropped onto the floral bedspread, grabbed a dainty pink pillow and began punching the stuffing out of it.

TOO BAD STANDING up to her loathsome ex-husband had exhausted Zora when she ought to be celebrating, Lucky thought. And how typical that Andrew hadn't bothered to consider how his actions might affect a woman coping with a multiple pregnancy.

What a joy to witness Zora bravely tackling that creep. How frustrating it had been these past months, watching such a smart, feisty woman repeatedly yielding to foolish delusions.

Yet, unfortunately, she might still forgive the jerk. If Lucky had learned anything about Zora, it was that her emotions regarding her ex-husband seesawed like crazy.

Once the babies were born, if Andrew showed any paternal instincts at all, her resistance would probably crumble.

That remark about wishing her kids had a dad like Lucky…for a split second, he'd wished the same thing. Then he'd faced reality. To her, the twins would always belong to Andrew.

Lucky sighed and clicked on the lamp in his bedroom, which was spacious enough for his video games and exercise equipment. During the day, when he opened the curtains, the sliding glass doors revealed a splendid view of the gray-and-green wetlands with their ever-changing tableau of wildlife. Tonight, by contrast, the lamp—on a ceramic base enlivened by a turquoise-and-black geometric pattern—bathed the room in a cozy radiance.

When he'd moved in here, Lucky had purchased several Hispanic-inspired accents, including the rainbow-striped serape draped across a chair as well as a ceramic Aztec calendar plaque that hung on the wall, its buff background covered with red-and-black designs. Although his family was three generations removed from its Mexican-Indian roots, Lucky valued his connection to ancient traditions. He'd worked hard to master Spanish both because of his heritage and to assist patients.

Overhead, the floor creaked, a reminder that Karen and Rod were awake. Lucky tried not to speculate about what they might be doing in Karen's suite. Whatever it was, he appreciated that they'd remained out of sight during the verbal fireworks with Andrew.

If only Zora had more energy, Lucky would have enjoyed sharing a late snack with her, teasing her across the table. It had been fun earlier tonight, figuring out how to persuade Vince to stay involved with Safe Harbor.

How sharp of Zora to note that Portia would do whatever was necessary to preserve her marriage. Especially since, in Lucky's observation, the woman's longing for a baby might tip the scales in favor of undergoing fertility treatments.

Whatever happened at Saturday's appointment, his involvement, if any, had to be discreet. Unhappily, he acknowledged that all this head scratching and cogitating might be for naught. It was possible that, upon receiving Cole's bad news, Vince would simply haul his wife out of there and bid Safe Harbor adios.

It would help to have a second set of eyes and ears. Zora had proven perceptive, and if she were around...

Why not? In addition to working weekdays, Zora filled in occasional evenings and weekends. Cole hadn't scheduled a full roster of patients for Saturday morning. Lucky could identify a few men due for ultrasounds who might be glad to move up their appointments. He'd request that Zora be assigned.

Satisfied with that plan, he changed into exercise clothes and switched on his elliptical machine.

WHILE GROWING UP, Zora had never had a close girlfriend. Her twin, who should have been her dearest pal, had become a rival because their mother had constantly pitted them against each other with criticism and shifting favoritism. By high school, Zora had transferred that competition to other girls as well, a view reinforced by Andrew's flirtations while they were dating.

Then she'd started working at Safe Harbor and, during the lowest period of her life, met Anya. She'd never understood why bubbly, popular Anya had defied the staff's general hostility to Zora and invited her to share an apartment, but she'd been deeply appreciative.

Sharing confidences and movie nights with a friend had been a revelation. A year later, after their rent increased and they moved into Karen's house, they'd continued to be best friends. Zora had been the first to learn that Anya was carrying Jack's baby, and it had been Anya who accompanied Zora to buy a pregnancy kit and discover her own impending motherhood.

Anya's marriage a few months ago, followed by the birth of her daughter, meant that Jack and little Rachel came first. Lonely again, Zora had drifted into Lucky's company, despite his irritating attempts to run her life. But now that her feelings toward him had changed, being around him was dangerous.

Zora needed a friend. And although Keely was far from the warm, cuddly type, she had a kind side. Late Tuesday afternoon, when Zora stopped into Dr. Brennan's office to inquire about paternity testing, the nurse immediately arranged for the doctor to order the lab test. She requested Andrew's email address and promised to send him the information, as well.

"The results take eight working days after you both provide blood." The older woman refastened the pink barrette in her hair. "Say, are you driving home with Karen today? I saw you arrive together. In case she has to stay late, I'd be glad to take you."

A hint of anxiety in the nurse's expression, as if the response really mattered, touched Zora. Not only did she need a friend, but Keely did, too. Also, Karen had texted that she'd be delayed about an hour and hoped Zora didn't mind waiting. The alternative—calling on Lucky—went against Zora's resolve to steer clear of him.

Dr. Brennan's warning about safety had resonated with her on the drive home yesterday, when she'd found that she could no longer reach the pedals without her baby bulge pressing against the steering wheel.

Thank goodness her housemates had volunteered to pick up the slack, and now Keely was joining in. "Actually, I *could* use a ride, if it's not too much trouble."

The lines in Keely's face softened. "Let's do it!" They arranged to meet in the medical building lobby in fifteen minutes, after Keely got off work. Zora had finished her shift an hour earlier.

At the lab, she had blood drawn. Thank goodness for the newer technique, which extracted fetal DNA from her blood plasma and compared it to the father's DNA. All the same, she'd be willing to bet that Andrew would complain about it. Too bad he didn't have to endure the doctor's poking, the morning sickness, the sleepless nights and the labor pains.

As she rose to leave with a small bandage on her arm, Zora supposed that women from the dawn of time had resented men for escaping the painful consequences of pregnancy. She wouldn't resent Lucky, who took care of her, though. But as he'd pointed out, these weren't his babies.

Recalling that she ought to alert Karen to the change in plans, Zora sent the other woman a text. When she reached the meeting place, Keely was already there, pacing. "Am I late?" Zora asked.

"No. I wasn't sure you'd be here."

"Why not?" Stupid question. Keely's low self-esteem spoke for itself. "I mean, you're doing me a favor. Of course I'm here."

"I'm parked in the main garage," the nurse said. "Is that too far? I could pull around."

"The exercise is good for me. And it's not far." As they set out at a slow pace, Zora asked, "Are you ready for the move this weekend? Did your landlord hassle you about the short notice?"

"Not after I explained the circumstances with my roommate." Keely brushed a speck of dust off her navy uniform. "And told him it was my birthday."

"It's your birthday?" Zora wondered about her new friend's age. It seemed rude to ask, though.

"Last Sunday."

"You should have mentioned it earlier! We'd have celebrated."

"Why?" Keely's eyebrows drew into a dark, straight line. "Turning fifty isn't anything to cheer about."

Well, she'd answered *that* question. "Every birthday is precious," Zora said as they passed a flower bed crowded with red, white and purple petunias. "Considering the alternative."

"What alternative?"

"Dying young."

Keely snorted, which appeared to be her manner of laughing. "Never thought of that." Halting at the garage's elevator, she pressed the button. "I can't afford to get old and sick, without a family to lean on." She punched the button again, although it was already lit.

"Fifty isn't old," Zora ventured.

"My mom was fifty when she had to go on disability." Keely's forehead creased. "I moved in with her after Dad died. She was forever consulting one doctor or another. Aches and pains, high blood pressure, swollen ankles. They ordered her to exercise and quit drinking. She insisted the booze was medicinal and that it hurt to move around."

"To move around at all?" Zora asked. "What did she do, spend the whole day on the couch?"

"Pretty much. I did the shopping and cleaning, while working full-time."

No wonder the nurse had a grumpy attitude. "Is she living?"

A shudder ran through Keely. "I'd rather not talk about it."

"I didn't mean to pry."

The elevator arrived and they rode up in silence. Had she offended Keely? Zora wondered. The woman had a reputation for being touchy.

At last the nurse spoke again. "I take it back. It's better for you to hear the truth."

"About what?"

They exited onto the third level. "About what happened to my mom," Keely answered. "I got arrested and lost my last job because of it."

That sounded shocking. Zora struggled to contain her reaction as they strolled between rows of vehicles. Behind them, an SUV pulled out cautiously. Ahead, a woman beeped open her sedan. Although there was a faint smell of exhaust, the garage's open-air design dissipated the fumes.

"What happened?" Quickly, Zora added, "Obviously, the police made a mistake." *Or did we agree to share our house with an ax murderer?*

"One morning Mom claimed she sensed a heart attack coming on." Keely's voice echoed off the hard surfaces around them. "She was constantly saying such things and complaining to the neighbors about how I neglected her. I'd missed too much work already, running Mom to doctors for no reason. I told her to call nine-one-one if her symptoms worsened."

"Oh, dear." Having grown up with a mother who insisted on being the center of attention at any cost, Zora empathized.

Keely's eyes glittered with tears. "After work, I found her stone cold in her favorite chair. A neighbor told the police I'd been abusing her."

"You must have been devastated." If Zora had ignored her mother's complaints and then she'd ended up passing away, she'd be overwhelmed by guilt.

"The clinic fired me as soon as they heard I'd been arrested." Keely paused at a bend in the row. "There I was, out on bail, handling my mother's funeral arrangements and terrified of being sent to prison."

"That's horrible." Zora's heart went out to the woman. "What did you do?"

The nurse sucked in a long breath before continuing. "Mom's doctors explained to the investigators that I was always bringing her in for one symptom or another. The district attorney decided not to prosecute."

"What about your job? Surely they offered to hire you back."

"I wouldn't work for those doctors again. They were cruel and unfair." Lifting her chin, Keely resumed walking. "I got a job at Safe Harbor. It was a community hospital in those days, before the remodeling. If the top brass now had any idea I'd been arrested for elder abuse, I doubt they'd put up with me."

"But the DA cleared you," Zora responded.

"Dr. Tartikoff hates me. If it weren't for Dr. Brennan…" Keely broke off. "Oh, no!"

She was staring at a boxy brown sedan with bumper stickers that read, Ask Your Doctor—Not Your TV Commercial, Cancer Cures Smoking, and Get Off Your Phone and Drive. The car also sported four flat tires.

"That's yours?"

Keely nodded grimly.

Four flat tires couldn't be a coincidence, Zora thought. "This is vandalism. We should call the police."

Keely shifted for a closer inspection. "They aren't slashed." Her jaw tightened. "Somebody let the air out. It's a nasty prank kids used to do to me in high school."

Keely had been bullied as a teenager, and someone was bullying her again. That aroused Zora's fury, along with her sympathy. "We should at least tell security."

"I'll call the auto club. They'll handle it." Keely swung toward her. "Please don't hold it against me that you have to wait."

"I wouldn't hold it against *you*!" Zora protested. "You're the victim here."

"I appreciate that."

Near the curve where they'd stood talking a moment ago, a motor started and a blue hybrid with a bike rack on top pulled out. It occurred to Zora that the perpetrator of this so-called prank might have lingered to observe—and enjoy—the consequences. "Do you recognize that car?"

"Afraid not."

In the dim light, Zora could see only enough of the driver to be fairly sure it was a man. Then, as the car drove off, she noticed that Keely wasn't the only staff member to display bumper stickers.

The one on the hybrid read, Psychologists Do It on the Couch.

Chapter Eight

"Thanks for calling me," Lucky told Keely after parking his car across from hers in the garage. She'd phoned to alert him to what had happened and asked if he could drive Zora home.

Reclining in Keely's rear seat with the door open, Zora eyed him askance. "You're both very kind, but I'm not a fragile doll."

Not a doll, but more fragile than she was willing to admit, Lucky thought, assessing her swollen calves and the weariness in her gaze. He was tempted to stroke a damp strand of hair from her temple, but her stubborn expression warned him against fussing over her.

"The auto club could take half an hour," Keely responded tartly to Zora. "Meanwhile you're breathing auto fumes. It's bad for the baby."

"She doesn't always exercise the best judgment," Lucky agreed.

"I'm right here! Please refrain from talking about me in the third person," Zora snapped.

Ignoring the complaint, he continued addressing Keely. "I notified security. A guard should be here soon to take a report."

Keely shrugged. "Fine. I have nothing else to do till the auto club arrives, but we can't prove Laird did this."

"Motive plus bumper sticker equals Laird," Lucky replied.

"*We* know that," Zora said. "But who else will believe a psychologist would stoop to such juvenile tricks over being bumped from a room rental?"

"Anyone who heard him squabbling with Keely in the cafeteria." Realizing that his comment might seem insulting, Lucky added, "No offense. I meant that he was the one squabbling."

Keely waved off the apology. "Don't bother soft-pedaling, Lucky. I'm tough. I butted heads with Dr. Tartikoff and survived, in case you forgot."

"How could anyone forget?" he teased. "You're a hero."

"Heroine," Zora corrected.

"You planning to argue with everything I say?" Lucky didn't mind, though, as long as she was safe. No sooner had he clicked off the call than frightening scenarios had rampaged through his head. What if the vandal had tampered with Keely's brakes and they'd crashed? "Keely, as a precaution, have the auto club tow your car to Phil's Garage to check the brakes and engine. I think they're open till seven."

"And spend my hard-earned money for nothing?" She shook her head. "I doubt the louse would go that far."

"I recommend playing it safe, but it's your decision." Reaching out, Lucky helped Zora rise.

He was glad he'd replaced his old low-slung coupe with a practical black sedan he could drive for years. And which didn't force a pregnant woman to pretzel herself into the front seat.

"All set?" He leaned inside to adjust Zora's seat belt.

A slap on the wrist knocked his arm away. "No touching the merchandise!"

"The seat belts can be tricky." He didn't attempt to assist again, however.

As a rule, Lucky preferred mild-mannered women, but

Zora's peppery manner had its pluses. Never boring, for one thing. Also, no stored-up complaints to be unleashed later. One ex-girlfriend had unloaded on him out of the blue, calling him an arrogant muscle head before breaking off their relationship. Until that evening, Lucky had believed they were doing fine.

Zora didn't hesitate to lob insults at him on the spot. In fact, *arrogant muscle head* was mild by comparison to some of her descriptive phrases. But at least he knew what she thought of him.

Yet despite her feisty spirit, she had a knack for landing in scrapes that begged for a rescue. If he had to move elsewhere for a job, who would show up on a moment's notice? *Somebody* had to take care of her.

As he navigated the curving ramp, Lucky glanced at the resolute mommy-to-be beside him. The full lips, the curving line of her lashes—spicy and sweet, like hot chocolate with a dash of cayenne pepper.

It occurred to him that he hadn't yet updated her on the latest twist to his plan. "Did you hear from the radiology scheduler about working Saturday morning?"

"No. Will I?"

He explained that he'd requested her. "You'll be nearby when the Adamses are here."

"To do what?" Zora demanded. "I doubt I'll get anywhere near them."

"I'd like your insight." Belatedly, he asked, "Do you mind?"

"I suppose not, but next time, ask me first." She flinched as, ahead, a car shot back into the aisle, blocking their path.

Lucky tapped the brake. "I saw it."

"Of course you did."

"You doubt me?"

"Always."

He chuckled. "About the Adamses, you might observe something I miss."

"Seriously?" When they emerged from the garage, lingering daylight glinted off the coppery highlights in her hair. "I thought you considered me a borderline drooling idiot."

"That's a wild exaggeration," he said.

"Which part—the drooling or the idiot?"

"The borderline."

She laughed. "I should have figured."

Heading south on Safe Harbor Boulevard, they crested a coastal bluff. Before them spread the shimmering harbor and adjacent stretch of sand. The arrival of October's cooler weather meant less traffic and smaller beach crowds, a situation Lucky relished.

Growing up, he'd been accustomed to his family's flat, landlocked neighborhood in LA. But after living in Safe Harbor, he'd never be satisfied being far from the expanse of the ocean.

Zora lowered her window. "That sea air smells wonderful."

"Better than exhaust?"

"Thank you for picking me up, if that was a hint." She stretched her shoulders. At this stage of her pregnancy, she ought to have regular massages to ease her discomforts. Lucky nearly volunteered, but the notion of running his hands over her body struck him as dangerously intimate, especially since she was sexy as hell.

"I'll drive you to and from work the rest of the week." He swung left onto Pacific Coast Highway. "Karen can alternate with me, but your hours are more in line with mine. Next week, after Keely moves in, I'll coordinate my schedule with her."

"You sure are bossy," Zora joked.

"Save your grousing for the Sunday meet-up." The residents of Casa Wiggins, as they referred to Karen's house, assembled once a week to review plans and problems.

"Keely will be there, which means I'll have an ally," she said.

"I'm used to you and Anya ganging up on me," Lucky replied calmly. "I can handle it."

"Handle it? You enjoy having women around even if they aren't bowled over by your tats," Zora said.

"That's true. Women share ideas and support each other more than most men do." Living in Casa Wiggins had taught him the value of friendships with the opposite sex. He'd grown up in a predominantly male household, with a strong-minded father and brother. His mom had been quiet by comparison, with a steady, low-key temperament. Lucky wished he'd had a chance to know her as an adult, but he'd lost her, a painful memory he'd rather not dwell on. "So, have you set up the paternity test?"

"None of your business."

He grinned. It felt normal to bicker with Zora. And he was glad she'd agreed to be at Dr. Rattigan's office on Saturday. Whether or not her input proved helpful, he was glad she'd be there.

THROUGHOUT HER SHIFT on Saturday morning, Zora stayed attuned to the activities in the rest of the office. Usually she only paid attention to her patients, but today she noted Lucky's familiar footsteps, registered the steady tone of his voice, and picked up the fact that Vince Adams was late. Very late.

Perhaps he and his wife had abandoned the possibility of a pregnancy under any circumstances, or decided to use a surrogate in San Diego. All of Lucky's planning could be for nothing.

He might have to leave. How would she handle that?

The sight of him at the garage on Tuesday had been far more welcome than Zora had expected. Since then, riding beside him to and from work, she'd been keenly aware of his powerful thigh close to hers and his muscular arms controlling the steering wheel. Fortunately, their habit of verbally poking at each other made it easy to hide her reactions.

Today, they'd arrived together but then separated to attend to their duties. The schedule kept Zora busy with a series of male patients.

During Zora's training, performing scrotal ultrasounds had required considerable getting used to. She had to adjust the patient's penis and scrotum, apply gel and move the paddle to obtain varied views.

During the procedure, the man often stared at the ceiling, responding to her requests as if commanded by a robot. Others cracked jokes to cover their embarrassment during the twenty- to thirty-minute procedure. Occasionally, she encountered a man whose sexual innuendos crept toward harassment. Her crisply professional manner and request for a nurse to observe had always sufficed to dampen the patient's ardor.

Zora preferred it when the wife accompanied her husband, which was the case with her fourth patient of the morning. A thin fellow in his late fifties, he gripped his wife's hand as Dr. Rattigan checked him before departing.

During the sonogram, a booming voice from the hall alerted Zora that Vince had arrived. Why did he trumpet every word? The man behaved as if everyone else, except a select few such as Cole, was not only invisible but also deaf.

Then a door closed and silence fell. Ominous silence. Scary silence.

Suddenly Lucky's faith in her powers of observation seemed ridiculously misplaced. His future and the expansion of the men's fertility program at Safe Harbor might be crashing and burning, and unable to see or hear what was happening, Zora had nothing to contribute. If only she could do *something*.

"How does it look to you?" The patient's question broke into her thoughts.

Instead of dwelling on the obvious fact that she wasn't a doctor, Zora tried diplomacy. "Dr. Rattigan will review the results with you personally. He takes great care with his patients."

"Yes, but…" The man broke off as his wife patted his shoulder. "I can't help worrying."

"We're almost finished," she told him. "Am I hurting you?" The procedure was painless unless the man was especially sensitive. However, asking the question ought to distract him from further inquiries.

"No, no. Thank you."

While she did observe some anomalies in the man's images, Zora wasn't qualified to interpret what they meant. Entering the medical field, she'd dreamed of helping others rather than simply clocking in to a routine job each day. And often, she *did* help them. She hoped that whatever was wrong with this patient could be put right.

The early loss of both her grandparents had inspired her interest in health care. She cherished memories of her mother's parents, who'd adored her and Zady. Unfortunately, they'd smoked, avoided exercise and ignored symptoms of heart and lung disease until it was too late for lifesaving treatments.

Zora didn't hold an exalted position like a surgeon, but she was part of a team that improved people's lives. She wouldn't trade her career for anything.

Once she'd finished the exam, she gently wiped off the conductive gel. "You can resume normal activities immediately."

"I think a leisurely lunch at Salads and More is in order," the wife said. "Don't you, honey?"

"How about Waffle Heaven?"

Their gazes locked. "Papa Giovanni's?" she countered.

"Done," he said.

Zora envied their easy rapport. How wonderful to have a spouse with whom you communicated in shorthand and who stood by you through life's ups and downs. The way Lucky did with her...but that was temporary.

"You may get dressed," she told the patient. "I'll be out of here in a minute."

"No hurry."

As she bent to retrieve a cord, her babies squirmed. Did they sense she was hungry? Pushing the cart out of the room, Zora smiled at the idea that her growling stomach had awakened them.

In the hall, she nearly ran into a bulldog of a man. His powerful frame corded with tension, Vince Adams scowled at the elegant woman beside him. Model thin, Portia Adams wore a svelte pink suit and to-die-for designer shoes. She struck Zora as determined and apprehensive.

Apparently the couple had finished their meeting with the doctor. Most patients avoided private discussions in the hallways, but not these two.

"You call that a compromise?" Vince demanded of his spouse. "I've told you I won't tolerate a surrogate! No stranger will be carrying my children. That's what I have a wife for."

In Portia's smooth face, only her eyes betrayed her fury. "I agreed to hormone injections and egg retrieval," she said in a low voice. "And I want a baby, well, almost as much as you do. But at my age, to take on a possible multiple pregnancy..." She shook her head and let the sentence drift off.

Spotting Zora, the billionaire maintained his glare for an instant before his expression softened. "Excuse me," Zora said, and eased the cart to the side to clear a path.

Instead of picking up the hint to exit, Vince bathed her in a smile. "What a beautiful sight you are, miss. Frankly, I find a pregnant woman's body irresistible."

"Thanks." Zora gritted her teeth, eager to escape.

Vince advanced toward her. "Your husband must be thrilled."

His wife glowered. Her twisting mouth conveyed resentment, but there was also a trace of fear in her eyes. Was she really that afraid of losing her husband?

"I don't…" Zora cleared her throat.

"She isn't married. She lives in that house with Rod," Portia snapped. She and Vince had attended Anya and Jack's wedding there when their daughters—Jack's cousins—had served as flower girls.

"You're not married?" Touching his thumb to Zora's chin, Vince tipped her face up. "The men around here must be blind."

Okay, that's enough taunting of your wife. She stepped back. "I'll remove this cart so you can get past."

"You do that," Portia snarled.

Before Zora could squirm farther away, however, Vince laid a meaty hand on her abdomen. "Boy or girl?"

"One of each." She wished she dared smack his arm.

To her dismay, he caressed her bulge with relish. Enjoying his wife's discomfort, or Zora's? Or both? "They're active little rascals, aren't they?"

Behind him, Lucky appeared. Mercifully, the interruption allowed Zora to break free and dodge behind the ultrasound equipment.

Unfazed, Vince addressed his wife. "Well, honey?"

The threat was unmistakable. If Portia didn't yield to his demands, he'd find a woman who would.

A long breath shuddered out of the socialite. "You don't care about the risk to me? Never mind, I already know the answer."

"You're exaggerating the dangers," her husband retorted. "You're only thirty-nine. Lots of women in their forties have babies."

Lucky intervened politely. "There is an increased risk, Mrs. Adams, but if there are no underlying health issues, it ought to be manageable with careful monitoring. You should discuss that with your doctor."

Her nose wrinkled. "What does a man know? He doesn't have to carry a baby."

Lucky didn't miss a beat. "We have excellent female obstetricians on staff."

Portia gripped her purse. "Do any of them perform in vitro?"

"Several," he said.

Vince faced Zora again. "Who's your doctor, honey?"

"Paige Brennan," she said.

"Dr. Brennan often works with in vitro patients," Lucky added. "You'd find her sympathetic, Mrs. Adams. She underwent fertility treatment herself in order to have her daughter."

That was none of their business, Zora thought. However, Dr. Brennan *had* spoken publicly about that aspect of her medical history.

"And she's married?" This appeared important to Portia. Did she think her husband so lecherous that he'd chase her obstetrician? Of course, he *had* just groped an ultrasound tech.

"Quite happily," Lucky assured her.

Portia gave a reluctant shrug. "I suppose she's acceptable."

Triumphantly, Vince draped an arm over his wife's shoulders. "Well done. Why don't we stay an extra day and attend that charity event you mentioned? I'll buy you a new outfit at South Coast Plaza."

"Not that I'll fit into it for long," his wife muttered, but quickly rallied. "Thank you. I suppose this might work out okay. A baby really will be a lot of fun."

To Lucky, her husband said, "Set up an appointment with Dr. Brennan. My wife can send you her schedule."

"Glad to." Judging by the light in Lucky's eyes, he was barely keeping a lid on his excitement.

While he escorted the wealthy couple to the front, Zora stowed the cart in its closet. On her return, she found Lucky performing a victory dance around the nurses' station. Fortunately for his reputation, there was no one else present.

He beamed at her. "I have no idea how you persuaded them, but you were brilliant."

"I didn't do anything." *Except let him grope my baby bump.* However, Zora supposed that Vince's behavior fell within what many might view as acceptable limits. A lot of people assumed—wrongly—that it was okay to touch a pregnant woman's belly.

"Too bad it's illegal to shoot off fireworks in a doctor's office." With a whoop, Lucky caught her. "We did it!"

Zora's discomfort evaporated. Close to him, she felt safe and sheltered. How easily she could forget everything and everyone, except… "Isn't Dr. Rattigan around?"

"He had to perform emergency surgery." Lucky rubbed his cheek over her hair. "He left right after talking to the Adamses."

"An emergency in urology?" Unlike obstetrics, the specialty rarely dealt with life-or-death situations.

"A patient suffered injuries in a car crash." Lucky mentioned a nearby hospital that handled trauma patients. "The lead surgeon called Dr. Rattigan to assist. Would you stop fidgeting and let me hug you?"

"That's nearly impossible in my shape." But Zora yielded happily as he wedged her against him. How strong he was, yet he held her with a tenderness that almost overwhelmed her.

Zora became acutely aware of his quick breathing. The discovery that she excited him spurred her passion. She floated in the heady scent of his citrus cologne, her nerve endings coming alive.

When Lucky's mouth brushed Zora's, her lips parted.

The flick of his tongue sent rivulets of desire streaming through her, and an answering moan burst from him.

She grabbed his shoulders and lightly rubbed her breasts over his hard chest. The sensations flaring through her were almost painfully intense. Lucky angled her tighter, his hands closing over her derriere.

The urge to bring him inside her, to merge with him, proved irresistible. "Let's find a place to be alone," she began, and then, shifting position, he stumbled.

"Oh, hell!" Lucky caught his balance against the counter, anchoring her against his hip. "Are you all right?"

"Delirious," she murmured.

Drawing in a ragged breath, he studied her in confusion. "We shouldn't be doing this."

"You're right. It's a terrible idea." Clinging to him, Zora didn't mean a word of it. "But as long as we've gone this far…"

"I never expected to get carried away." His thoughts seemed to turn inward. "What's wrong with me?"

"Wrong?" Zora bristled.

"I never lose control this way," Lucky said. "Considering your condition and our situations, I apologize."

"For what?" Oh, why was she torturing herself by prolonging this conversation? Zora wondered. She'd acted impulsively, and clearly Lucky didn't like the way he'd reacted. What a control freak! "Never mind. Forget the whole thing."

"That's a good idea." He sounded as if he was struggling for composure. "That wasn't how a gentleman behaves."

"If you apologize again, I'll slug you."

He laughed, an unexpected rumble that rolled right into her heart. "That's my Zora." A bout of hard breathing reawakened her hope, but he sucked in a lungful of air and held it. "Okay. Better."

"Than what?"

He ignored the question. "Since I inveigled you into working today, let me buy you lunch to celebrate."

Was that his interpretation of what they'd been doing—celebrating? Slapping him would have been totally satisfying. Still, she was starving. Why reject a good meal? "Where did you have in mind?"

"There's a new vegetarian Chinese restaurant I've been meaning to check out."

Zora loved Chinese food. "Do they serve anything besides tofu?"

"Kung pao mushrooms, according to the online menu. Deep fried, with a tangy sauce. And more, I'm sure."

"You're on." The heat in her body hadn't exactly dissipated, but it had faded to her normal pregnancy-enhanced high temperature. As for Lucky, he'd evidently banished whatever desire he'd experienced.

I guess I'm nowhere near close enough to perfection to suit him.

As common sense reasserted itself, Zora recalled his previous comment about her babies. Never mind Lucky's withdrawal from her—he didn't, couldn't and never would accept these babies as his own.

She was glad they'd stopped. Going any further would have been yet another in a long line of mistakes she'd made with men.

Gathering her possessions, she waited until Lucky locked up, and they sauntered out together. Friends again, nothing more.

Which was obviously how they both preferred it.

Chapter Nine

Lucky enjoyed the Sunday meet-ups at Casa Wiggins. He'd learned from his parents, who'd run a small business, that organization was the key to controlling your destiny. In the eight months since the household had formed, the gatherings had enabled the group to stay on track through changes in occupants and in individual situations.

This afternoon, despite his awareness that the future was more of a meandering path with speed bumps than a superhighway, he felt optimistic about his plans. Thanks to whatever diplomacy Zora had exercised toward the Adamses yesterday, all systems appeared to be a go.

Relaxing in his favorite armchair in the den, he sipped white grape juice from a glass. As usual, Rod and Karen had chosen the couch, with their sock-covered feet propped on the worn coffee table. Zora preferred the straight chair, which was easier for a pregnant woman to get in and out of. That left newcomer Keely, who clomped down the staircase to join them.

"Am I late?" she asked. "I had trouble finding the laundry room."

"It's the narrow door next to the garage," Zora said.

"I thought that was a closet."

"Everybody assumes that," Karen assured her. "Don't hesitate to ask where things are."

"You're running laundry already?" Rod fingered his short, graying beard. "You just moved in."

Karen nudged him. "Not our business, dear."

"It's a harmless question."

"I'm a strong believer in hygiene." Crossing the den, Keely lowered her sturdy frame onto the remaining armchair. "How often do we clean and who does what? With a pregnant woman on the premises, we must be vigilant about germs."

Don't tell me she's a germophobe. Lucky rolled his eyes, then caught Zora's stern gaze and subsided.

"We have a rotating schedule. I'll give you a copy," Karen promised. "Feel free to swap chores with anyone who's willing."

"Surely Zora doesn't have to handle chemicals or do heavy work." Keely slid to the edge of her seat, no doubt having discovered that otherwise she sank into the depths of the chair. Lucky decided to ask Karen about replacing the cushion. They maintained a household fund for that sort of thing.

"We have a great system," Rod said. "We chain pregnant women to a wheel in the basement so they generate electrical power."

Keely's jaw dropped.

Zora, who was seated closest to her, murmured, "There is no basement. I handle dusting and other light chores."

Their newest housemate nodded. "I forgot that Dr. Vintner is famous for joking."

"Dr. Vintner? Anytime you see me with my shoes off, you can call me by my first name." Rod wiggled his sock-clad toes on the coffee table.

Karen presented a few more house rules, such as putting snack plates and cups in the dishwasher rather than accumulating them in the sink. "And no sticking them in the oven because you're in a hurry," she tossed in Zora's direction.

"Anya and I only did that once," she replied cheerfully. "It's not our fault someone turned on the oven without checking if there was anything inside."

"Oh, dear." Keely clutched her hands together. "What if I do things wrong?"

"We'll toss you out," Rod replied.

"Where would I go?" To Lucky's astonishment, Keely regarded Rod in dismay. The woman needed to develop a sense of humor.

Zora reached over to pat the newcomer's hand. "You'll get used to our silliness. Are you still upset about what happened on Tuesday? That must have thrown you off balance."

The older nurse's head bobbed. What had happened on Tuesday? Lucky had to search his memory before he dredged it up. "You mean that nasty prank with your tires? What's the connection?"

"She was bullied in school," Zora said fiercely. "I understand what it's like to be an outsider. Keely, nobody will bully you in this house. If they do, we'll toss *them* out."

"You bet," Karen affirmed.

"I'll cheer while Lucky does the physical tossing," Rod said.

"No problem." Lucky was pleased when Keely responded with a smile.

What a spirited defense Zora had mounted, he thought. As for that outsider business, he bore a share of the responsibility for being tough on Zora. When she first arrived at the house, he'd considered her a heartless predator who'd hurt Stacy. Gradually, he'd forgiven her, and since she'd stood up to Andrew, he'd come to respect her. As for her empathy toward Keely, that demonstrated her kind heart.

The doorbell rang. "I'll get it." With unaccustomed speed, Rod hurried to the door. Lucky heard low voices and then caught a heavenly whiff of garlic, tomato sauce and cheese.

Rod returned toting three large pizzas. "My treat. This will be my atonement for cracking jokes at Keely's expense."

"Three pizzas?" the nurse replied in astonishment. "That's too much for five people."

"Don't you like leftovers?" Lucky asked.

"And it *is* Sunday," Karen said. "People might drop by."

"I'll set out the paper plates and stuff." Rod was definitely acting out of character today—for a reason, as Lucky knew.

To distract Keely, and also because he cared about the answer, Lucky said, "I've been wondering about the timetable for the in vitro process. It's not a situation Dr. Rattigan and I usually deal with. We have a patient who might be affected."

"I'm happy to answer, but are we finished discussing house rules?" The dark-haired woman glanced from him to Zora to Karen.

"Yes, unless you have more questions," Karen said. "Don't let Lucky rush you."

"I'm fine. Is everyone interested in hearing about in vitro?"

"I am," Zora said. She, too, was probably wondering how long it might take before Portia and Vince saw results.

Keely launched into a spiel that she must have heard Dr. Brennan deliver to patients a hundred times. "Depending on the phase of the woman's cycle when you begin, the whole process can take about a month."

"Fantastic." Noting her puzzled reaction, Lucky quickly added, "Go on."

With increasing confidence, she complied.

ZORA LISTENED ATTENTIVELY, though that was partly for Keely's sake—the other woman obviously craved reassurance that she belonged here. The subject matter was familiar to her, but she wanted a clearer picture of how things might progress for the Adamses.

The first stage, Keely noted, was the administration of medication to stimulate the ovaries, almond-size glands that flanked the uterus. Normally, only one or two eggs matured each month, but drugs could produce the simultaneous maturing of multiple eggs. This improved the chances of harvesting and fertilizing enough viable eggs.

Keely was explaining step two, harvesting, when the doorbell rang again. From the table at the farthest part of the den, Rod plummeted toward the front door. No one attempted to rise; if they had, he'd have bowled them over.

A creak of the door, and excited, girlish voices filled the air.

"Daddy!"

"Grandma Helen, give Daddy the cake before you drop it."

"I'm not that decrepit," responded the dry voice of their grandmother.

"I'll get it." Lucky, who'd ordered the cake, went to join the new arrivals.

Until yesterday, the plan had been for the Adamses to return to San Diego that same day. However, Portia had been lobbying to stay over at a hotel so she and Vince could attend an exclusive charity concert and reception tonight, and in his expansive mood, he'd agreed. Helen Pepper had promptly called her former son-in-law to inform Rod that she and the girls could join the household for dinner tonight.

As long as they were having guests, Lucky had decided this was a good chance to show their new roommate what a great group she'd joined. Zora couldn't wait to see her reaction to the cake honoring Keely's birthday.

"I smell pizza!" cried thirteen-year-old Tiffany Adams, her red braids bouncing on her shoulders. "Ooh, where are my manners? Hi, everybody. Zora, you're *huge*!"

"The twins have grown since August." Last summer,

Rod's daughters had visited often, since their parents had rented a beach house nearby while Vince underwent surgery.

Eleven-year-old Amber followed shyly. "Have you picked names?" she asked Zora.

"Not yet."

"Gee, they brought dessert." Grinning, Lucky carried in a castle-shaped pink box bearing the logo of the Cake Castle. "Is somebody having a birthday?" No one responded. "Or did someone have a birthday last weekend?" he asked with feigned innocence.

Keely shook her head. "You don't mean me, do you?"

"Hmm. Let's check."

As Lucky passed Zora, she studied his physique appreciatively. His tattoos and muscular build used to remind her of her stepfather, a foul-mouthed ex-gangbanger. Now, she knew that Lucky was nothing like that loser. In fact, as yesterday's encounter had proved, she found him tantalizingly attractive.

Last night, she'd lain awake, her brain defiantly replaying the incident. What if he hadn't stumbled? How far would they have gone? At this stage of pregnancy, making love wasn't wise. Just as importantly, if he'd repeated his insistence afterward on holding out for Ms. Perfect, she'd never have forgiven him.

It was fortunate for Zora's sanity and their friendship that they'd stopped. If only her dreams would quit defying her common sense. But then, where a man was concerned, this was familiar territory.

Carefully, Lucky opened the box to reveal the cake. "It says, 'Happy 50th Birthday, Kelly.' Doggone it! I spelled 'Keely' for them twice!"

The amazement on Keely's face touched Zora's heart. "It's for me?" She approached the table and stared at the icing inscription. "But being fifty isn't worth celebrating. I'm over the hill."

"You consider fifty old?" The girls' grandmother patted Keely's shoulder with an arthritic hand. "My fifties were my best years. Still, I don't mind growing older, not when it means watching these darling girls grow up."

When Zora reached fifty, she reflected, she'd have twenty-year-old twins. For a second, she visualized them with dark hair and smooth olive skin, like Lucky. But of course, they'd either have her reddish hair or Andrew's blond coloring.

Amber joined the small group around the cake. "It's beautiful. I want a rainbow on my next birthday cake, too."

Tiffany took out her cell phone. "I'll snap a picture so we don't forget."

"Hang on, honey." Rod caught his daughter's wrist. "You said Vince snoops through your stuff, right?"

"Oh, rats." The girl scowled. "He'll demand the details of who it was for and where we saw it."

"He's mean." Amber's frown mirrored her sister's.

Keely looked puzzled. "I don't understand."

"I'll explain while we eat," Rod said.

Over pizza, they filled in the story of how Vince had wrested his stepdaughters from the man who'd raised them and attempted to banish Rod from their lives.

"Surely the Adamses must suspect that they visit Dr. Vintner." Keely had chosen a tight spot at the table's corner, declining the place of honor toward which the others had tried to direct her.

"They sort of know but pretend they don't," Amber said. "I'm sure Mom has an idea."

"It's like a game," Tiffany put in.

"Despite the satisfaction of flipping them the bird, we shouldn't be forced to sneak around." Rod spoke from the head of the table, the seat Keely had bypassed. "I spent my life's savings fighting that man in court."

"If you run into Mr. or Mrs. Adams, please don't mention that you met their daughters," Karen told Keely.

The nurse swallowed a bite of food. "I won't. I promise."

Lucky met Zora's gaze. They were both thinking the same thing, she gathered: that it was fortunate Karen had issued the warning before Portia became Paige Brennan's patient. Keely would be running into her often.

"The girls might be in town more often now that my daughter's trying for another baby," Helen observed.

"Mom and Vince plan to rent a beach cottage again, closer to the medical center," Tiffany filled in.

"What about your education?" Rod asked. "You'll have to switch schools."

"I don't mind," Amber answered. "The kids at my school are snotty."

"Besides, private schools bend over backward to accommodate you if your parents give a big donation." Tiffany's cynical attitude bothered Zora until the girl said, "Oh, yeah, and Mom and Vince promised a gift to the animal shelter here, because it's our pet project."

"Pet project?" Rod waggled an eyebrow.

"Tiffany made a pun!" Amber giggled.

"And you volunteer there, Dad," his older daughter said. "It'll be cool for Vince to be funding *your* favorite charity without realizing it."

Zora wondered how Vince would treat his future genetic child or children. And how would he behave toward his stepdaughters? Perhaps he'd mellow out. She doubted it, though.

After wiping her hands on a napkin, Zora rested them on her bulge. Thinking about daddies reminded her that Andrew had had his blood drawn on Wednesday. The results might arrive by the end of the week, not that she had any doubts about them.

"Let's cut the cake." Tiffany jumped up to clear the table.

They'd polished off the better part of two pizzas, with leftovers to stock the fridge. Karen, with her usual efficiency, would jot on the cardboard box the number of slices allocated to each resident. Despite occasional carping in the early days—accustomed to living with other guys, Lucky had pushed for the first-come-first-served approach— they'd found that this method maintained the peace.

Karen produced birthday candles, which Lucky lit using a strand of spaghetti in lieu of the fireplace torch they'd misplaced. Then they sang, lustily if raggedly, a round of "Happy Birthday."

Keely stood with hands clasped and eyes sparkling. As they finished amid cheers, she sniffed. "I can't believe you guys did this."

"You're part of the family now," Karen said.

"Hurray for Keely!" added Tiffany, who hadn't had a clue to the woman's identity until today.

Amber sidled up to the newcomer and took her hand. "Being fifty sounds good. I bet nobody bosses you around."

Too choked up to speak, Keely nodded.

Rod did the honors, at Karen's request. "This is as close as I get to performing surgery," the anesthesiologist said as he divided the cake. "Keely, which piece do you prefer?"

"Take the one with the rainbow roses on it," Amber advised.

The nurse bestowed a quavering smile on the youngster. "If you recommend it."

"I do."

Across from her, Zora watched Lucky beam at the cozy tableau. He was deriving as much joy from the situation as if they'd thrown *him* a surprise birthday party. What a natural father he'd make.

Whenever he found the perfect time and the perfect woman.

THAT WEEK, KEELY, Karen and Lucky alternated providing rides for Zora. Since Rod's unreliable car was in the shop, he tagged along, too. That led to hilariously nonsensical discussions, and kept Zora from feeling that she was imposing too heavily on her friends.

On Friday, the radiology scheduler assigned her to the same-day surgery unit on the fourth floor of the hospital. Busy with clients, Zora only glanced at her phone in rare free moments in case of urgent voice messages or texts. There was one asking her to call Keely, which she presumed meant a change in whoever was driving home from work.

During her break that afternoon, Zora headed for the fourth-floor staff lounge, eager to put her feet up and answer messages. Waddling around a corner, she nearly collided with her ex-mother-in-law. Her hand shot out to the wall for support.

"Sorry." Betsy braced as if preparing to catch her. "Are you okay?"

"Sure." Zora removed her hand. "I, uh, don't usually see you here." The nursing supervisor's office was on the fifth floor, although Betsy's duties might take her anywhere in the building.

"I was looking for you." The older woman walked with her toward the lounge. "Radiology said you were on this floor today. Can we talk?"

Zora occasionally chatted with Betsy about crocheting or mutual acquaintances when they ran into each other, but the older woman didn't usually single her out this way. "Is there a problem?"

"Hold on." Opening the lounge door, Betsy scanned the interior. It was empty, Zora saw. The vending machines and kitchenette appeared in pristine condition, no doubt tidied since lunch. "Good. We're alone."

Why was that good?

Zora settled on a couch. Without asking, the older woman brought her a cup of herbal tea from a machine.

"You ought to stay hydrated," Betsy said from an adjacent chair. "In fact, you should be on maternity leave."

"I'm saving as much of my time as possible for after the twins are born." Zora hoped she could hold out another few weeks.

"You don't have to go through this alone." Betsy's green eyes, augmented by her spectacles, zeroed in on her. "I wish you'd felt comfortable confiding in me, although I understand your reluctance."

"Andrew told you that he's the father?" He must have received the lab results of the paternity test today.

"Yes, he did." Worry lines deepened in Betsy's square face. "That's why I wanted to talk with you. I believe you ought to hear his plans."

He was up to something already? With a sinking sensation, Zora conceded that she should have expected this. She sighed. "Hit me with it."

Chapter Ten

Trying not to panic while Betsy gathered her thoughts, Zora stretched out along the couch. As usual, she'd been floating on what Lucky had once termed the river of denial. She hadn't bothered to consult her attorney to prepare for Andrew's stratagems, such as ducking child support payments. She'd let matters drift, while he'd apparently prepared a trap.

Betsy spread her hands in dismay. "There's no way to soften this. He might sue for custody."

"What?" Zora would have bolted to her feet except that she was long past the ability to bolt anywhere. "How ridiculous! He doesn't want the kids." More objections tumbled through her mind. "And since Lin walked out, who does he think would care for them on the wildly improbable chance that he won the court battle?"

"Me," her ex-mother-in-law said. "He asked me to raise the babies. I guess he assumed I'd leap at the chance, because he knows how much I would love grandchildren."

Zora stared at her, stunned. Never in her most bizarre dreams could she have concocted such a scheme. Finally she found her voice. "You told him no, right?"

"Without a moment's hesitation."

"Can you please explain what he was thinking?"

Betsy rolled her eyes. Zora didn't recall ever seeing her ex-mother-in-law do that before. "I long ago gave up on understanding my son. Sadly, he takes after his father. In case you don't remember Rory very well, my ex is a total narcissist."

"He seemed distant." As a teenager, Zora didn't recall exchanging more than superficial greetings with Andrew's father. When she and her old flame reconnected ten years later, his parents had divorced.

Rory hadn't attended their wedding, a lovely ceremony followed by a reception she'd rather forget. Zora's mother had drunk too much, waxed maudlin about her baby girl, then vomited on the buffet table.

"I asked Andrew why the hell—excuse me, heck—he'd sue for custody," Betsy said. "He claimed you'd tricked him into fathering kids just so you could hit him up for support, and he doesn't plan to let you win. His words, not mine."

The man had incredible nerve. "He lied to me about reconciling so he could seduce me. That's how I got pregnant." Embarrassment heated Zora's cheeks. "I was naive. The fact that he didn't bother with protection struck me as a sign that he was serious, because we'd been trying to have kids. I had no idea until later that he'd had a vasectomy and believed he was sterile." Then she realized what she'd revealed. "I'm sorry to drop that on you."

"Oh, my son already did," Betsy said wryly. "He was almost gleeful as he informed me these are the only grandchildren I'll ever have. He failed to grasp that I can be their grandmother without depriving them of their mom."

Betsy was running a risk by bringing Zora the truth—she might offend her son and she had no guarantee Zora would grant her access to the kids. "Of course you're their grandmother. I'd love for you to be part of my children's lives, and mine, too."

The other woman glowed with relief. "I've always felt as if you were my daughter."

"Me, too." In high school, Zora had often relied on

Betsy for comfort and advice, since she couldn't trust her own mom. A rush of happiness ran through her, to be on intimate terms with Betsy again.

"I doubt any court in California would hand my son sole custody," Betsy added. "If you need me to testify about how unfit he is, just say the word."

Zora swallowed hard. "You're a saint."

"Oh, I have my faults." With a quirk of the eyebrow, the grandmother-to-be inquired, "To change the subject, I've been wondering—have you picked names?"

Suddenly, Zora had an answer. Half of one, anyway. "The girl will be Elizabeth."

Betsy's eyes widened. "For me?"

"Absolutely." Also, Zora liked that name.

"Count on me as your number one babysitter." The nursing supervisor appeared about to explode with joy. "Do me a favor, would you?"

"Sure. What?"

"Don't name the boy Andrew." Quickly, Betsy added, "Not to deprive my son. It's because being a junior can cause confusion."

"Understood." The reason scarcely mattered; Zora wouldn't name her little boy Andrew for a million dollars. Well, maybe a million. And then she'd use a nickname.

Outside in the hall, she heard light footsteps approaching. In midafternoon, there hadn't been much traffic in this wing. Same-day surgeries were conducted early enough for patients to recover by late afternoon, and most were still recuperating at this hour.

Zora glanced at her watch. "Sounds like we're about to have company, and I'm due to see a patient."

"If you need help arranging for leave, let me know."

"Thanks, but..."

The door opened and a woman peered in, reddish-brown hair rioting around her head. "Excuse me. I'm supposed to be interviewing with Dr. Davis on the fourth floor but I can't find his…"

Utter and total silence fell over the lounge. Because the face looking back at Zora was her own.

FOR LUCKY, FRIDAY afternoons could be crammed with last-minute patients or, like today, extremely light. Cole had accepted several extra surgeries and ordered him to reschedule office appointments.

Since Keely had to work late, Lucky was happy to switch their arrangement and drive Zora home, but she wasn't answering her phone. Not unusual—she might be with patients. After determining that she'd been assigned to the same-day surgery unit, he decided to grab a snack at the cafeteria and stop by the fourth floor to try to catch her in a free moment.

Emerging from the stairs, he had a moment of disorientation when he spotted her down the hall. Why was Zora wearing street clothes, and— Wait a minute—what had happened to her pregnancy?

Then he remembered that Dr. Davis was in town to interview nurse candidates and find a place to live. He'd be joining the staff at the beginning of November, a few weeks from now. Zady, one of the nurses slated for an interview, must have been confused about which fourth floor was involved—she'd gone to the hospital instead of the office next door.

"Miss Moore?" Lucky didn't like to shout, but she failed to hear him. Instead, with no nurses' station in sight, she headed for the next best thing, the staff lounge.

After opening the door, she stood frozen, her shoulders rigid. A warning bell rang in Lucky's head.

Standing behind the slender figure with hair a shade lighter than Zora's, he peered inside. Sure enough, staring at Zady with her mouth open was the shocked face of his housemate.

From the recesses of his suddenly sluggish brain, Lucky dredged up the words, "I can explain." But before they reached his vocal cords, a third woman spoke from the side.

"What a pleasure to run into you, Zady." Betsy Raditch, he realized, must have met Zora's twin when the girls were teens.

While she and Zady exchanged greetings, Lucky tried wafting apologetic vibes in Zora's direction, but she ignored him. It hadn't occurred to him the sisters might come face-to-face today. In the event that Zady landed the job, he'd assumed there'd be plenty of time for him to break the news once it was no longer a matter of confidence.

He wondered what issues had separated the sisters. If someone unexpectedly threw him together with his brother, there'd be hell to pay. But their split had occurred under unusually traumatic circumstances.

He snapped to attention, hearing Zady say she was in search of Dr. Davis's office. "That's on the fourth floor of the building next door," he said.

"Dr. Davis?" Betsy's forehead wrinkled. "Oh, the new urologist. I heard you were vetting the nurse candidates, Lucky."

Two pairs of large gray eyes fixed on him. "You must be Mr. Mendez," Zady said.

Zora mouthed the formal name—*Mr. Mendez?*—and grimaced.

He'd have to wait until later to provide the details of his involvement. "I'll escort you," he told Zady, adding for Zora's benefit, "I'm driving you home today. Keely has to stay late."

"Fine," she growled. Since he'd brought her in this morning, she knew where he'd parked his car.

The twins regarded each other hesitantly. "I don't understand why—" Zady began.

"What're you doing—" Zora started.

They paused, radiating mistrust. But something else too, Lucky thought. Hope, perhaps?

"You ladies should talk," Betsy said. "But right now, I gather there are people waiting. Do you have each other's phone numbers?"

Both heads shook. While they input the numbers in their mobiles, Zady said, "I'm staying at the Harbor Suites. Let's meet when you finish work." She provided her room number.

"I don't mind driving you over there," Lucky put in, although he didn't expect to receive any thanks.

"Okay." To her twin, Zora said, "Good luck with the interview, I guess."

"Yeah, thanks. I guess."

Lucky accompanied Zady to the elevator. In answer to her query, he said he was one of Zora's housemates, which seemed to puzzle her even more.

She had a lot of questions, including why Zora was renting a room in a house instead of living with her husband. Lucky told her he'd leave that for her sister to answer.

How strange that Zady didn't know her twin was divorced. But then, he had no idea whether his brother was married or had kids, or what Matthew had been doing these past sixteen years. The only cousin with whom Lucky kept in touch diplomatically avoided the subject.

Occasionally, Lucky had considered searching online to scope out Matthew's status, but that risked arousing old fury and resentment. Better to let sleeping dogs lie. He'd fought hard to regain his equilibrium after his brother lined up the rest of the family against him. Now that he'd found a second home among friends, why revisit the past?

Unlike Lucky, these sisters had a mother with whom Zora was in contact, and Zady probably was, too. Why hadn't she passed along vital information such as Zora's marital status?

Lucky expected to learn more in due time. Although he might catch a scolding from Zora during the drive, it would be worth it.

AFTER ZADY DEPARTED, Zora struggled with a wave of bewilderment and regret. Had it really been nine years since they'd fought? Her outrage had long ago dissipated. But according to Mom, Zady did nothing but boast about her happy marriage and loving children while dropping snide remarks about Zora. Yet if Zady was content, why did she want to leave Santa Barbara? And why apply for a job at the medical center where Zora worked?

Betsy broke the silence. "I know you two are estranged, but I've never heard why. Granted, it's none of my business. Still, I noticed during high school that whenever I saw the two of you laughing and having fun together, the next thing I heard, you were fighting. I hope you've outgrown that."

Zady used to play nasty tricks on Zora, after which she not only feigned innocence but leveled accusations at *her*. It would be childish to dredge that up, however. "A lot of siblings fight."

"I can't speak from experience. My brother was much older, more like an uncle, and I only had one child." Betsy arose. "You have a patient scheduled?"

"Oh, that's right!" She'd forgotten to watch the clock.

"I hope you'll talk to your attorney about Andrew," Betsy added.

"I will." After a quick hug, Zora departed, her mind buzzing with the latest developments.

Good thing she'd have Lucky to review them with after work. Right after she read him the riot act.

ON THE SECOND level of the garage, Zora approached the familiar black sedan where Lucky was comfortably ensconced, apparently listening to music. On the sloped ramp, she paused to observe him.

With his dark coloring and dramatic cheekbones, Lucky had drawn her attention as soon as he'd started working at Safe Harbor, about a year after she had. While she'd considered him handsome, he wasn't her type, and she'd been married to Andrew.

Later, when Cole fell in love with Stacy, loyalty to his doctor—although Cole had never indicated any animosity toward Zora—had turned Lucky into her fiercest critic. She'd refused to let him scare her out of moving into Karen's house, however, and over the past months, he'd changed.

When he'd reviewed the nurses' applications for Dr. Davis, why had he chosen her twin as a finalist—to create trouble? Surely he hadn't eliminated more qualified applicants for Zady's sake, though. Perhaps she simply deserved to be considered.

"Oh, good, I caught you." Rod's voice yanked her from her reflections. "My transmission's on the fritz again. Blast that car. I'm definitely trading it in."

"Hi, Rod." He must have received Lucky's permission to join them—how else would he know the car's location? Zora mused as they strolled side by side to the car. "We have a stop en route," she informed the anesthesiologist. "My sister and I are having a, well, touchy reunion."

"Fine with me." He opened the rear door for her. Inside, the blare of country music cut off. "I'd offer to sit in the back but it's safer for you to be there."

"Thanks." Zora hefted her body inside.

"I'll drop you at the Harbor Suites," Lucky said from the front. The one-bedroom suites rented by the day or week. "I'll pick you up again after I take Rod home."

"That's a lot of driving," Zora said.

"It's ten minutes in each direction." Rod closed her door

and hopped into the front, adjusting his fedora to avoid it bumping the roof.

Lucky put the car into reverse. Although tempted to ask why he'd approved her sister as a potential colleague, Zora wasn't keen on reviewing the whole business in front of Rod.

Fortunately, he was preoccupied with the latest developments concerning his daughters. Helen had reported that the girls were starting at their new school next week, and that Vince had insisted both of them play soccer, which Tiffany hated.

When the youngster begged to study dance instead, her stepfather had said he was tired of her complaints. He planned to send her to boarding school in Switzerland when she entered high school the following autumn.

"Her mother doesn't bother to defend her," Rod said angrily. "If the girls are too much trouble to have around, they should let me raise them."

"Not much chance of that, is there?" Lucky observed.

"I wish there were. Karen would welcome them. They can have my room." Rod and Karen had begun spending nights together in her master suite.

Vince would never let go of anything he considered his, Zora reflected. The thought of the billionaire sent a shiver through her. The memory of him groping her abdomen repulsed her. Well, he'd accomplished his goal of arousing his wife's jealousy, and hopefully that was the end of that.

They pulled into the parking lot in front of the Harbor Suites. Among the vehicles, she spotted license plates from neighboring states: Arizona, Oregon, Utah, Nevada. Patients undergoing fertility treatments often rented rooms here.

Lucky halted in front of the office. "You want me to stay? If you're worried, I will."

What a sweet offer. "I'll be fine."

"If we hear screaming, we'll turn around," Rod joked.

After Zora got out, Lucky lowered his window. "I'll pick up food on my way back."

Why was he acting so nice? In self-defense, Zora supposed. "Chinese would be good. Or Italian."

"Okay."

Despite her brave words, dread filled Zora as the car drove off. Years of silence between her and Zady loomed in front of her like an abyss.

Still, she was curious about her sister's situation, she conceded as she followed a sidewalk between the one-story buildings. And if Zady ended up at Safe Harbor, they'd have to reach an accord sooner or later.

Halfway across the grassy courtyard, past a few squatty palm trees, Zora spotted the room number Zady had given her earlier. Taking a deep breath, she knocked on her sister's door.

Chapter Eleven

Inside, footsteps rushed across the carpet. Zora's pulse sped up as the door opened and she stared into a face at the same height as hers, a face that mirrored hers, from the freckles to the wary expression.

A memory sprang up. For their senior prom, they'd accidentally bought the same dress and, after a horrified moment, they'd dissolved into laughter. Rather than quibble about who should return the gown, they'd coordinated the rest of their outfits, as well. Their classmates had assumed they'd deliberately picked matching dresses and shoes, while they'd confounded their mother. It had been rare fun.

"Hi." Zady moved aside, admitting her to an austere living room furnished with a nondescript sofa and reproductions of seascapes on the walls.

Zora noted a can of soup in the kitchenette next to the microwave. If that was her sister's idea of dinner, Zady was either on a diet or short of money. Well, according to their mother, her sister had three children, enough to strain any budget.

"Let's get one thing straight." Zady's words sounded rehearsed.

"What's that?"

"If Dr. Davis offers the job, I'm accepting it."

It hadn't occurred to Zora to suggest otherwise. "That's fine. I won't beat around the bush, either."

"Okay." Hands clenched, Zady waited by the couch.

Ignoring the sofa, Zora chose a hard chair. "Regardless of what Mom may have claimed, here are the facts. Right before Andrew and I finalized our divorce, I slept with him because I believed he still loved me. Then he married his new girlfriend. Now I'm pregnant with twins, which I plan to keep."

Zady dropped onto the couch, eyes wide. "You're divorced? Mom said your husband dotes on you. Takes you on luxury cruises, showers you with jewelry—I'll admit, it didn't sound like the Andrew I remember from high school, but—you're carrying twins? Are they identical?"

"No. A boy and a girl."

"That's good. Maybe they won't hate each other."

The remark brought an unexpected pang. "Do you hate me?" Zora asked.

"No, I assumed…" Zady broke off.

Although Zora was dying to learn more about her sister's feelings, first things first. "Why did you apply to Safe Harbor? What about your husband and kids—are they moving here?"

"Dwayne and I never married." Zady kicked off her low-heeled pumps. "And I don't have kids, unless you count his three obnoxious children who treat me as their personal maid."

The world was shifting on its axis. "Are you still living with him?"

"No." Her twin didn't look up, apparently fascinated by her stocking-clad feet. "He's like Dad, forever cheating."

"So is Andrew!"

"And I was too stubborn and proud to admit it until he forced my hand."

"Me, too."

They regarded each other across the coffee table. Zora could almost have laughed, except the situation was pathetic.

"You didn't finish your story," Zady said. "Since Mom obviously lied about everything, I'd like to hear the truth. She said Andrew sought you out during his first marriage because he'd never stopped loving you. Is that right?"

"No. We bumped into each other at our high school reunion. Wish you'd been there."

"Are you kidding? I was too embarrassed about my situation with Dwayne. Go on."

Zora poured out the tale of how Andrew had dumped Stacy, then cheated on Zora. "In high school, you told me he sneaked around with other girls," she recalled. "I'm sorry I accused you of being jealous."

"And I'm sorry I didn't listen when you warned me that Dwayne was a jerk."

"I guess I did." With all that had happened since, Zora had forgotten that she'd tried to steer her sister away from him. She'd had more sense about Zady's choices than her own.

"You were right not to trust him." Zady waved her hands in a gesture Zora recognized, because she did it herself when agitated. "Not only didn't he marry me, Dwayne refused to have kids. He stuck me with his unholy brood during their vacations, claiming I should learn to love my 'stepchildren.' He used the free time to play around. I closed my eyes to it, until his new girlfriend got pregnant."

"How did he react to that?"

"Oh, he's excited about being a proud papa again." Bitterness laced Zady's voice. "I wouldn't count on it lasting, if I were her."

"Andrew didn't refuse to have children with me," Zora said. "We were trying for a pregnancy before he met, well, *her*. I stopped taking birth control pills during our last year together, but nothing happened until after we separated."

"Hmm…that timing is weird." Zady frowned.

"I agree, but it's not as if he tricked me while we were married. I'd have noticed if he was wearing a condom."

"If I've learned anything, it's that a manipulative jerk will do stuff you'd never dream of."

"Maybe, but I can't imagine how..." Zora stopped. "Oh, Lord, you're right. I may have just figured it out."

"What?" Her sister leaned forward.

Zora smacked herself in the forehead. "After I stopped taking the birth control pills, he claimed he threw them out. I was touched. But what if he crushed them into my food?"

"For an entire year?"

"There was a three-month supply in the drawer." He'd become solicitous about her diet, preparing breakfast to be sure she ate properly for their future children. "As my husband, he'd have had no problem refilling the prescription."

"But a year's a long time." Zady appeared both disgusted and fascinated.

"He went out of town on occasion," Zora conceded. "But we weren't having sex during his absences, either. And I marked our wall calendar with what I assumed were my most fertile days. I was frustrated when he always claimed to be exhausted after he got back from a trip right when we should have been making love. I should have suspected something."

"What a lot of trouble. He could have sneaked off and had a vasectomy without telling you," Zady said. "The scar's usually very small."

Zora threw up her hands—just as her sister had done moments earlier, she realized. "Why be straightforward when you can be manipulative? Andrew enjoyed playing games and tricking people. Or I could be wrong about this."

"I'm sure it must be illegal to dose a person with prescription medication without her consent," Zady added.

"That wouldn't bother Andrew." Nothing could be proven now, Zora supposed, even though the scenario explained a lot about Andrew's behavior. "Well, eventually he did have a vasectomy, but he assumed his sperm count was zero after a month. Now he's attempting to punish me for demanding child support."

"How?"

She described the plot to sue for custody and persuade his mother to raise the kids. "Betsy gave me all the details earlier today."

"That's what you were discussing in the lounge?" Zady slapped the coffee table. "How could we have fallen for such jerks? Why didn't we tell them to go to hell a whole lot sooner?"

"Gullibility. Love," Zora assessed. "And pride. Mom kept bragging about how perfect your life was."

"I cried on her shoulder practically every week. And she regaled me with stories of how happy you were." Zady blushed. "I couldn't give up on Dwayne because I refused to let you win."

"I felt the same way." Zora winced at how easily they'd been maneuvered. "How long do you think she's been lying to us?"

"Since we were born?"

Zora recalled Betsy's observation. "You're right. Whenever we had fun together, you could count on something happening to mess it up."

"Such as you borrowing my new sweater and ruining it." That incident had triggered their final blowup while they were in college. The squabble over a minor transgression had deteriorated into cross accusations and name calling. Soon afterward, Zady had left town with Dwayne.

"I didn't touch your sweater," Zora said. Had their mother really stooped that low? Obviously, yes. "You didn't borrow my earrings and lose one, either, did you?"

"No." Zady buried her face in her hands, then peeked between her fingers. "How sick, that she was jealous of her own children being close."

"Mom destroyed your sweater and my earrings so we'd fight." Zora struggled to grasp how cruel that had been.

"She always had to be the center of attention," Zady noted.

"That's why we were sitting ducks for Andrew and Dwayne," Zady said. "We grew up being manipulated."

"Imagine how she'll react when she learns we're on good terms again." Zady blew out a long breath. "She'll do anything to split us up."

"Let's not tell her." As she spoke, Zora could almost hear Lucky coaching her in the background, urging her to avoid her old traps by changing her behavior.

"How can we avoid it?"

"If we confront her, she'll start scheming," Zora pointed out. "We should say as little as possible to her."

A smile lit Zady's face. "That'll drive her crazy."

"Exactly."

"But if I land the job at Safe Harbor, she'll realize we must be talking," Zady said.

"We can say we only see each other around the building. End of story."

"She'll interrogate her old friends who live here."

"If she has any, they won't know anything." Zora's only contact from her mother's generation was Betsy, who was too smart to play those games.

"Wow." Zady regarded her in admiration. "That's both simple and diabolical."

"Let's function as a team. Full disclosure about everything."

"Done!"

Across the coffee table, they high-fived each other. For nearly ten years, Zora had been missing part of herself. "I'm only sorry it took us this long to come together. I'm glad my kids will have an aunt."

"Me, too." Zady regarded Zora's bulge wistfully. "How

will you raise them alone? If I'm living here, I'll pitch in, but I'll be working all day, too."

"There's day care at the hospital. And I have friends." Zora would be lost without her supportive household. "They've already raised money for a part-time nanny." Her phone buzzed with a text. Glancing down, she saw Lucky's message. "And there's my ride, waiting out front."

"Is that Mr. Mendez?" Longing shaded Zady's expression. "He's very kind. And he admires you, I can tell."

This was interesting news. "Did he say so?"

Her sister shook her head. "Not specifically. It's the way he looks at you, and how he avoided revealing too much about your situation while he walked me to the office building. He was protecting you."

"As a friend." Yet what if it meant more? Was it possible Lucky was falling in love with her, too? But he'd never abandon his ideal scenario, let alone agree to raise Andrew's children. "I shouldn't keep him waiting."

"Of course not."

Rising, Zady held out her hand to boost Zora. Then they flung their arms around each other.

"We're back," Zady crowed. "Twins forever!"

No more allowing others to separate them. "I hope, hope, hope you get the job."

"Me, too."

Amazement filled Zora as she eased out of the suite and along the path. How wonderful it would be to have family in town, especially the person who ought to be closest to her.

She couldn't wait to share their conversation with Lucky.

As the October darkness gathered, Lucky drummed his fingers on the steering wheel. He had no idea what to expect from Zora—complaints? Fury? But his tension also derived from another matter.

Rod's complaints on the drive home had reminded him that Vince and Portia were barreling ahead on their pregnancy project. Once his wife had yielded, the billionaire hadn't wasted a moment. Since his treatment needed to be coordinated with hers, Lucky was able to follow their efforts.

After reviewing Portia's up-to-date medical records and confirming that she was in excellent health, Dr. Brennan had started her on medication to adjust her cycle. Once her eggs ripened, Dr. Rattigan would remove sperm from Vince's testes. Then her eggs would be harvested and injected with her husband's sperm.

Despite the most advanced treatments available, there were no guarantees. The average pregnancy rate per cycle was in the 20 to 35 percent range, but Portia's age lowered her chances. It was likely to take more than one cycle for the implantation to be successful.

But the men's program had to win Vince's support sooner than that. Cole had informed Lucky yesterday that the bankruptcy court was expected to approve the vacant dental building going on sale by mid-November. Several doctors' groups had expressed interest in the space.

Without that building, expansion of Lucky's program would be difficult. No comparable facility with offices and labs existed in Safe Harbor. As for constructing a new one, the logistics of acquiring land and receiving government approvals made that option prohibitive.

So if Vince delayed too long, Lucky might have to choose between using the degree he'd worked so hard for and leaving his friends. Friends who, as he'd become keenly aware, filled the lonely places in his soul.

The creak of the car door jerked Lucky from his reverie. Zora swung onto the seat beside him. "Have you met Dr. Davis? Is he a nice guy? Do you think he'll hire Zady?"

She sounded excited rather than angry, thankfully.

"You're in favor of her landing the job?" Lucky switched on the ignition.

"Yes!" She drew the seat belt across her body. "It would be fantastic to have my sister here. My kids could grow up with their aunt, and besides, we belong together."

Things had gone well, then. Lucky smiled. "I was afraid you'd take my head off."

"For keeping her interview a secret?" Zora issued a growly noise. "You deserve it! But no."

"Her application was private." Moot point, now that Zady had revealed the facts to her sister. "I only met Dr. Davis briefly, but I like him. As for who he'll choose, the other candidates are also excellent. Tell me, what did you and Zady discuss?"

"Everything! It's incredible." Any concern that she'd keep Lucky in the dark vanished as she described Zady's selfish boyfriend and the similarities in their romantic experiences. The revelation about Andrew's possible abuse of her birth control pills was outrageous, but, unfortunately, in character for the louse.

Navigating along Coast Highway toward their house, Lucky maintained a leisurely speed to prolong the conversation. Beside him, Zora radiated an almost sexual intensity. The curve of her cheek invited his hand to stroke it, but he gripped the wheel tightly.

It wasn't safe to get distracted while driving. And once he touched her, he might not be able to stop there. He'd recognized his susceptibility to her that day in the office, when they'd nearly gone too far.

If it were only a question of the two of them, maybe... but he refused to risk giving his whole heart to a family that he couldn't be sure he could provide for. And what if Andrew decided he wanted to be a father to the twins? How he could be sure he'd never let Zora or the children down when, ultimately, control could be snatched out of his hands?

He'd made a workable plan for the future, one he could live with and sustain, and right now that plan did not allow for a wife and kids. No matter how he felt about Zora, ultimately he'd have to move past it.

"I understand better now why we fell for Mom's crap." She adjusted the seat belt, which tended to creep up on her abdomen. "Our mother pulled stunts to pit us against each other, and we bought it. She's been lying to us for years, convincing each of us that we were in competition."

She'd never told him that before, only that her mother was an alcoholic and her stepfather a bully. Lucky hadn't pressed for details, partly because he and Zora hadn't been close until recently, and partly because he resented it when people probed his own past. "I had no idea she was fomenting trouble for you."

"Neither did I. It's because of her that Zady and I had our last big blowup." She outlined how their mother had destroyed their property and tricked them into blaming each other. "It was cruel. We've lost nearly a decade. Our mother must be a— Who was that Greek guy that fell in love with his own reflection?"

"Narcissus."

"That's it! She's a narcissist."

"You should cut her off," Lucky said. "It's what she deserves."

"We're putting up a united front," Zora responded. "Keeping her at arm's length will drive her nuts."

"Don't play games." Zora's assertiveness was new and likely fragile. She could easily be sucked back into self-defeating behavioral patterns if she continued to speak to her mother. "You should have nothing further to do with her."

In the faint light as they passed a streetlamp, he saw frown lines pucker her forehead. "She's our mother."

"To feed her ego, she groomed you to be patsies," he retorted. "Don't let Zady persuade you to stay involved with your mother. It's great that you've reconnected with your twin, but not if she's a bad influence."

"My sister isn't a bad influence!" Zora's shoulders stiffened. "And how we handle our mother is none of your business."

"It is if you spiral back into codependency," he said. "Because I have to live with you."

She appeared about to argue, but curiosity won. "What's codependency?"

"Codependents try to save loved ones from the consequences of their own actions because of a misguided sense of loyalty." After reading about the subject in a class on substance abusers and their families, Lucky had been astonished at how often he spotted the behavior in acquaintances and patients. "They feel guilty and trapped and blame themselves for the other person's faults, as you did with Andrew. You're a raging codependent, Zora."

"Now you're claiming I have a mental defect?"

"I'm helping you keep your life on track." To him, it seemed obvious.

"Wow, and I thought you'd changed." Far from heeding his warning, she was working up a head of steam. "Mr. Judgmental."

"It's for your own good." Lucky winced at the banality of his words. "That may be a cliché but in this instance, it's true."

"You expect me to abandon my mother and my sister because that's what you did with your brother when he crossed you."

Anger flared. Her situation didn't remotely compare to Lucky's. "You have no idea what separated Matthew and me."

"I know you're estranged from your entire family," Zora snapped. "He offended you, so Mr. High and Mighty Luke Mendez rejected him and everyone who stood by him."

"I had very valid reasons."

"What reasons?"

"He said vicious things no one could forgive, and obviously he doesn't regret it, since he never apologized."

"What did he say that was so terrible?"

"I have no intention of repeating it." Although Lucky had been only eighteen, his older brother's cruel words remained seared into his brain. *It's your fault our parents are dead, and you cheated me of my inheritance. You should be in prison.*

Matthew had repeated the lies to their aunts and uncles, who had barred Lucky from family gatherings. After several attempts to reason with them, he'd decided to cut himself off from them entirely.

True, he'd messed up, badly. He'd never forgive himself for the mistakes that had hurt their parents. But he hadn't caused their deaths and he would never, ever cheat anyone.

"Maybe he's changed," Zora suggested.

"I've led a fulfilling life without my brother's destructive influence," Lucky replied tautly. "You should do the same with your mother."

"I'm not you." As they entered the driveway, Zora said, "Thank heaven."

"I agree."

"You do?"

"If you were like me, you'd be the first pregnant man in history."

She didn't laugh. Too bad. Lucky had been aiming to lighten the mood.

He supposed she believed that his promise not to nag her over Andrew also applied to the rest of her behavior. But to him, she'd come so far in the last couple of weeks, he didn't want to see her lose her newfound confidence and self-esteem.

If he'd annoyed her, it was worth it.

Chapter Twelve

Angered by Lucky's arrogance, Zora avoided him over the weekend. She kept busy exchanging photos and messages with Zady, and went grocery shopping with Keely, although the nurse's insistence that she buy organic foods ran up the bill.

It was more than Lucky's haughty attitude that disturbed her, she realized after a second night of troubled sleep. In her dreams, her angry father raged at her, Zady and their mom. After his sudden death from a heart attack when she was twenty-two, Zora had pushed those ugly memories aside, preferring to dwell on her father's kinder, more loving moments. But the discovery of this rigid, unforgiving side of Lucky's nature had reawakened them.

Not that she hadn't expected this, at some level. After all, he insisted on the perfect family situation, including, presumably, a wife who arrived without baggage. No messy old relationships, and no children.

Yet, foolishly, she'd allowed herself to count on Lucky, to venture close to loving him, as if he might find it in his heart to change.

Why do I keep falling for the wrong guy?

If she entered another intimate relationship, Zora vowed to do it with her eyes open. Until then, once she discovered a man's fatal flaw, she'd distance herself from him, no matter how much her heart ached. And Lucky's fatal flaw was his intolerance for other people's flaws.

On Monday, she consulted Edmond regarding child support. He promised to file for half of Zora's unreimbursed medical and other maternity expenses.

"Once the babies are born, their father will be entitled to visitation and possibly shared custody," Edmond advised from behind the desk in his fifth-floor office. "That doesn't necessarily mean he gets physical custody half the time, but he will have an equal say in decisions about their care."

Much as she would hate sharing the children with their unworthy father, Zora supposed that she could hardly refuse contact. "He can't take them away from me, though, can he?"

"That would be extremely unusual," Edmond assured her. "He would have to prove that being around you endangers the children, such as if you were using drugs."

"I'd have to prove that for him, too, to block shared custody?"

"That's right." He adjusted his glasses. "In a case like this, it's tempting to try to cut him out. However, the courts have ruled that it's in a child's best interest for him or her to have a relationship with both parents."

Privately, Zora doubted it. However, she understood that laws and legal rulings had to apply to a wide range of cases.

When Lucky drove her home that evening, she suppressed the instinct to spill out what she'd learned from Edmond. She hadn't shared Betsy's confidence about Andrew's latest ploy, either.

He's judgmental and pitiless. The words played through her mind on a repeating loop, warning her to maintain a distance.

So when the silence weighed too heavily, she broached the merits of organic foods, a topic that interested him.

Lucky explained that he was vegetarian more for health reasons than for philosophical ones, although sparing animals' lives was a bonus. The man didn't appear to notice that she was withholding any information of a personal nature.

On Tuesday morning, Zora was assigned to perform sonograms at Dr. Brennan's office. Her obstetrician urged her to stay off her feet as much as possible, and Keely brought enough cups of tea to double her already frequent trips to the restroom.

While every patient was important and required her focus, Zora sensed an undercurrent of excitement building among the staff in the late morning. The reason became clear when she wheeled her cart into an exam room where Portia Adams lay on the table. Her auburn hair highlighted with chestnut and gold strands, she wore a hot-pink hospital gown that she must have brought with her. The only other person present was the doctor.

Lips pressed into a thin line, Portia watched Zora with a flare of the nostrils. Was the woman still jealous? *How sad*, Zora thought as she readied her equipment.

She was thankful for Dr. Brennan's narrative during the sonogram. "Everything's right on target." Seated on a stool, the doctor crossed her long legs. "We may be ready to harvest your eggs by the end of next week. Are you experiencing mood swings?"

"No more than usual," Portia said tartly. "How soon will my pregnancy start to show? I'm on the committee of a Christmas charity ball for the animal shelter and I must be sure my dress will fit."

Dr. Brennan blinked. She must have heard a lot of odd questions, Zora mused as she removed the probe, but this one evidently caught her by surprise.

"If you become pregnant on the first try, you'd still only be a few months along by Christmas," she said. "Maternity clothes probably won't be necessary. However, for comfort, I recommend a loose-fitting style."

"That's what I meant," Portia said. "I just want to buy the right style."

When Keely entered the room, Zora started to wheel her equipment out. As she opened the door, she heard the nurse say to Dr. Brennan, "Mr. Adams has arrived. Shall I send him in?"

"Wait till I straighten my gown," Portia responded. "How's my hair?"

It was too late for her to retreat, Zora realized as the door closed behind her, leaving her alone in the hallway. And there he was, his large frame nearly filling the corridor and forcing her to halt.

"Well, well." Despite the expensive cologne and expertly cut hair, Vince had a sleazy air. "If it isn't the lady with the earth-goddess body."

"Your wife's waiting for you, Mr. Adams." Zora peered past him, hoping to spot another staff member. No such luck.

"Has anybody told you lately how sexy you are?" The man's low voice might not carry into the closed examining room, but Zora wished it would. Then surely Dr. Brennan or Keely would respond.

"Thank you." She rattled the cart. "Excuse me."

Vince's expression hardened. "I'm an important man around here. You should consider the advantages of keeping me happy."

What nerve! "That's hardly appropriate for a woman in my condition." *Or any woman in any condition.*

"There are other ways of pleasing a man," he muttered close to her ear.

Zora's stomach churned. "I have a patient waiting." Not true, but she didn't care. And neither, she gathered from Vince's unmoving stance, did he.

Mercifully, noises from inside the examining room fi-

nally penetrated his awareness. From his pocket, he produced a business card and scribbled a phone number on the reverse. "My cell." He stepped aside. "Call me."

Zora stuck the card in her pocket and hurried away. As she stored her equipment, her hands were trembling.

What was she going to do? The only way to be sure of avoiding the man in the future was to complain about his disgusting behavior. Sexual harassment violated hospital policy, but it was his word against hers.

No, not entirely. She'd attended a talk by the hospital's staff attorney, Tony Franco, highlighting the seriousness with which such claims were regarded.

But if the hospital hassled Vince, that ended any chance of a donation. His wife could transfer to a doctor in San Diego. Was it worth it? The man hadn't tried to *force* Zora to do anything against her will. He'd merely been unpleasant.

Still shaky, she headed for the elevators. In her pocket, she imagined the card covered with slime. Best to discard it immediately. Except, what if she needed to prove that he'd propositioned her? Zora resolved to let her emotions settle before reaching a decision.

After washing her hands—it was impractical to take a shower, despite the icky emotional residue left by her encounter—she went to the cafeteria. In her present mood, she'd rather avoid Lucky, and was glad to see no sign of him. Instead, she spotted Betsy at a table with Lin. The third Mrs. Raditch must have had her follow-up appointment with Dr. T this morning.

With her tray of food, Zora joined them. At nearby tables, heads swiveled and voices murmured. Didn't these people have anything more substantial on their minds?

Betsy pulled out a chair. "I'm glad you're here."

"Me, too, Grandma," Zora said lightly. "Lin, how are you?"

"Dr. Tartikoff found nothing suspicious," the young woman replied.

"That's wonderful." Zora hesitated to raise another sensitive topic. Lin's next comment spared her that.

"I have talked to the attorney you recommended." Lin placed her dirty tableware neatly atop her empty plate. "He suggests an annulment on the grounds that Andrew defrauded me."

"By pretending to be a human being?" Embarrassed at her bluntness, Zora glanced apologetically at Betsy. "Sorry."

"No offense taken." Her ex-mother-in-law's mouth quirked.

"He lied about the vasectomy," Lin answered. "He claimed he had it during your marriage and promised to reverse it for me."

"Instead, he had the vasectomy *after* you got engaged." Which meant he didn't intend to reverse it, in Zora's opinion.

"Mr. Everhart called me after he contacted Andrew's attorney. It appears he will agree to the annulment," Lin said. "It will be as if the marriage never occurred."

How strange that, a month ago, this was what Zora had dreamed of, she mused as she ate. No more third wife. Instead, her sympathies now lay with Lin. "Will you stay in America?"

The other woman sighed. "I called my parents and they are eager for me to return."

"I wish you all the best," Betsy told her. "I hope you meet a man who deserves you."

"I doubt I will have as nice a mother-in-law," Lin said.

"How sweet." Betsy gazed at her pensively before turning to Zora. "If I may ask, what's the latest on your sister?"

Zora sketched the situation to her rapt audience. When she finished, she spotted Lucky standing with his tray, gazing around. A tremor ran through her at the reminder of the difficult choice she faced about Vince.

If she told him what Vince had done, how would he respond? Was it possible he'd think Zora had invited the other man's attention? Or, with his rigid insistence on propriety, would he pressure her to report Vince's harassment?

"You look pained," Betsy said. "Are you okay?"

"It's heartburn." Zora didn't dare reveal the truth. As nursing supervisor, Betsy would be obligated to inform the administrator.

"I must go." Lin stood, and Betsy, who'd finished her meal, did the same. "It is good to meet you again, Zora."

"Congratulations on your annulment." Zora almost regretted that Lin was returning to Hong Kong. She'd grown fond of her fellow sufferer.

How had Andrew managed to trick three intelligent women into loving him? Zora recalled Lucky describing her as a raging codependent. It must be a common condition.

He strode over, nodding to Betsy as she departed. Keely headed in their direction as well, her strong-boned face alight.

As the housemates settled, Keely spoke first. "I have great news! Mr. Adams plans to announce his donation soon."

Lucky gave a start. "He told *you*?"

"Dr. Brennan and me." The nurse transferred her dishes from the tray to the table. "He said the hospital is arranging a press conference. They're rushing the announcement because the dental building is going on sale."

Lucky slapped his thighs. "Fantastic!"

"He won't be able to jerk us around anymore," Zora burst out.

"Absolutely." Lucky's dark eyes sparkled. "Once he donates the money, we can stop worrying."

"That's right." This development reinforced Zora's resolve to keep quiet. Losing the billionaire's support at this point would be devastating, and unnecessary. But what a relief that she only had to hold out for a little while longer.

"He and his wife were joking about whose name will go on the building," Keely added. "Just his, or both of theirs."

"I can guess which side Vince was on." It wouldn't surprise Zora if the man's monstrous ego required the hospital to paint an enormous portrait of him covering the front of the structure as well. She wondered how hard it would be to sneak out and ornament it with a large mustache, blackened tooth and eye patch.

"They can put their daughters' names on it, too, as far as I'm concerned." Lucky popped open his carton of milk. "We can call it the Everybody Who's Ever Been Named Adams Medical Building."

Zora tucked into her tapioca pudding, relishing the creamy texture and vanilla flavoring. The rest of her meal had gone down almost untasted.

Idly, she wondered why a number of other diners were sneaking glances at them. Betsy and Lin had left, and Keely hadn't spoken loudly enough for her disclosure to carry above the general chatter. Lucky's enthusiastic reaction might have drawn attention briefly, but the staring seemed to be increasing.

"What do you suppose Laird's up to?" Lucky indicated a compact male figure perched triumphantly on a chair while the listeners at his table leaned toward him attentively.

Keely stiffened. "He keeps smirking at me."

"That's the third table he's bestowed his noxious presence on." Lucky didn't miss much. "The man already took his petty revenge on you for beating him to the rental. What more does he expect to gain?"

A lull fell across the room as a group of prominent physicians—Dr. Tartikoff, Cole Rattigan and hospital administrator Mark Rayburn—entered from the patio dining area. Into the quiet, Laird's words—*her own mother*—jangled like an old-fashioned telephone. The administrator frowned at him before glancing in Keely's direction with a troubled look.

The nurse paled. "Oh, my gosh! How did Laird find out?"

"Find out what?" Lucky asked.

As Zora tracked the path of the doctors toward the exit, the answer hit her. "He must have heard Keely and me talking in the garage. He was lurking in his car to watch her discover the flat tires."

"What were you discussing?" Lucky queried.

"It's…personal." Keely closed her eyes, her face a study in anguish. Fury rose in Zora at the jerk who'd inflicted this on her.

Or could she be mistaken? "That was two weeks ago. I don't understand why Laird would wait till now to attack you."

Keely's shoulders slumped. "I do."

"Would somebody please enlighten me?" Lucky said, clearly growing frustrated.

"I'll start at the beginning." Keely described her mother's death and the false allegation of elder abuse made against her that she'd eventually been able to disprove. "On Monday, Dr. Brennan asked if I was involved in any legal proceedings. I told her I wasn't. She apologized for jumping to a conclusion."

"I don't follow." What did Dr. Brennan have to do with Keely *or* Laird?

"Neither did I, but it worried me," Keely admitted. "When I pressed her, she said her husband had asked if I was still her nurse. That's all, but it reminded me that he's a private detective."

"Laird must have hired him to dig into your background." Unbelievable. To go that far, the psychologist had to be deadly serious about driving Keely away.

"I'm sure the detective informed him that the charges had been dropped." Lucky scowled in Laird's direction.

"People already dislike me." Keely shuddered. "Did you notice Dr. Rayburn's expression? Laird must have gone to him."

"You haven't done anything wrong," Lucky insisted.

"When the old community hospital was sold, we all went through a rehiring process and background check." Keely's thick eyebrows formed an almost straight line. "They asked if we'd ever been charged with a crime. I put down 'No.'"

"Well, you weren't," Zora protested.

"But I was arrested," the older nurse said. "Some people assume that's the same thing."

"Let's call an emergency house meeting tonight," Zora said. "We'll help you deal with this. Okay?"

Keely nodded. Lucky tilted his head in agreement, but in view of his judgmental tendencies, Zora was prepared to stand up to him tonight. She might not be able to take on Vince Adams, but Lucky Mendez was another story.

Chapter Thirteen

Due to schedules and commitments, it was nine o'clock before the household assembled in the den. Lucky had filled in Karen and Rod, who were ready for action.

"I'll chip in for an attorney." As usual, Rod shared the couch with Karen. "Legal costs can grind you under. That might be part of Laird's agenda."

Lucky assumed the anesthesiologist's view was colored by his own experience with the legal system.

In her chair beside Zora, Keely twisted her hands. "Do I *have* to get a lawyer?"

"It might be premature. Has anyone from Human Resources spoken to you about this?" Karen asked.

Keely's straight dark hair slashed the air as she shook her head.

"Edmond offers a free consultation." Lucky studied Zora's reaction, and was disappointed that she gave no sign of how she felt. He'd been hoping to learn that she'd met with Edmond herself to set the wheels rolling against Andrew.

How frustrating that she'd barely spoken to him since their disagreement on Friday. When Lucky had urged her to shut out her mother and, if necessary, her sister, he'd never expected her to shut *him* out instead. He had to admit, he might have gone overboard where her sister was concerned. Although he didn't entirely trust Zady's influ-

ence, she meant a lot to Zora. And family was precious—
unless they performed a demolition act on your happiness.

But he hadn't had a chance to soften his position in
the face of Zora's stonewalling. Talk about driving a person crazy.

Talk to me. Not this instant, of course, but he wished
she'd stop avoiding his gaze.

This afternoon, he'd confirmed that the hospital had
scheduled a press conference for a week from Thursday
to announce a major donation. Lucky should have been
exultant, but his emotions refused to cooperate because he
couldn't share his happiness with Zora. After all, expand-
ing the program would allow him to stay in Safe Harbor.
It angered him that she seemed willing to forgive Andrew
almost anything, and him nothing.

However, they had a more immediate matter on the
floor. Lucky seized the initiative. "We should advise Dr.
Rayburn about Laird's behavior. Don't forget he let the air
out of Keely's tires—"

"We can't prove that," Zora interrupted.

"You saw his car at the scene." Lucky had checked, and
her description, including the bumper sticker, fit Laird's
vehicle. "He also hired a private detective to snoop into a
staff member's background for revenge."

"We can't prove that, either," Rod observed. "And if
there was a hospital policy forbidding nosiness, we'd all
be out of a job."

Keely hunkered down, arms crossed protectively. Zora
scooted her chair closer to Keely's as an indication of sol-
idarity.

"Laird's an embarrassment to the hospital." Lucky
had developed a disgust for the man since witnessing his
drunken, lecherous behavior more than a year earlier during Elvis Presley night at the Suncrest Saloon. "I'm willing to march into Dr. Rayburn's office and demand he put
a stop to this bullying. Who's with me?"

Zora laid a hand on her bulge, which was rippling beneath her maternity top. "Before we start painting protest signs, let's hear Keely's opinion."

"Fine." From his easy chair, Lucky fixed his attention on the older nurse.

She cleared her throat. "I'd like to run this by Dr. Brennan."

"Tomorrow?" Lucky urged.

"She's busy on Thursdays," Keely said. "She has surgeries scheduled."

"She can spare five minutes." The doctor had already showed concern for her nurse when she mentioned her husband's question, hadn't she? "Get her on your side."

"I don't want to drag her into my personal business."

"Don't let Laird intimidate you." With adrenaline pumping through his system, Lucky felt the urge to jump to his feet and pace.

"Oh, quit pressuring her," Zora snapped. "Keely has a right to handle this however she chooses."

"You mean through avoidance?"

Karen raised her hands. "Peace, everybody. As Zora said, this is Keely's decision. We're the backup team."

"Yeah, okay." How had this conversation become an argument between him and Zora, anyway?

Keely released a breath. "I'll talk to my doctor tomorrow."

"Good for you," Zora said.

How come she didn't give Lucky any credit? He'd pushed Keely to do exactly that.

"Are we finished?" Rod asked. Everyone nodded. "Before we break up, you'll all be pleased to hear that I plan to replace my broken-down junkmobile. Any suggestions?"

"A hybrid," Zora said. "You'll save a fortune on gas."

"Consult the online ratings," Keely contributed.

"I'm considering a sports car," Rod added. "Possibly red."

"Watch out. The cops will ticket you every time you edge a few miles over the speed limit." Lucky had heard that from officers who'd chatted with him during his stint as an ambulance driver.

"I should drive a gray SUV instead?" Rod demanded. *"Boring."*

"Buy a car that seats five or six," Karen recommended. "So you can transport the girls and their friends."

"If only."

"Speaking of guests, that brings us to the topic of Thanksgiving," their landlady said, deftly seizing control of the discussion. "How about cooking our dinner a day or two after the holiday? There'll be more chance your daughters can join us."

They speculated on how next week's announcement might affect Vince and Portia's holiday plans but weren't able to reach a conclusion. As for the dinner, scheduling it on a Saturday was fine with Lucky. He usually volunteered to serve food at a homeless shelter on the holiday.

Amid yawns—they were an early-rising bunch—the meeting dispersed. Aware that Zora customarily drank a glass of milk before bed, Lucky watched for his chance and slipped into the kitchen when she was alone.

He noted her cute freckled nose, red hair that frizzed by day's end and legs propped up on a nearby chair. Choosing a chair around the corner of the small table, he reached for her nearest foot.

"Hey!" Zora attempted a glare that bore a strong resemblance to a squint.

"Tired?" Lucky drew his thumb along her instep.

"It's been a busy day." She patted her belly for emphasis.

She should go on maternity leave before she collapsed and delivered in a hall. However, Lucky was trying to reconnect with her, not irritate her. "How're things with Betsy and the third Mrs. Raditch?" he ventured.

"Fine."

He gritted his teeth. As he lifted her other foot and massaged it, her body relaxed. Progress! "Any word from your sister about the job?"

"No." She sank lower in her chair, eyelids drooping.

As Lucky stroked her feet, he noted they were puffy. It must be agony for her to stand all day. *None of your business.* Great—he didn't have to speak any longer; her responses sprang up automatically in his thoughts.

"It must be interesting, working in a different department each day," he said.

"Oh, there are a lot of repeats," she murmured, and fell silent.

"Doggone it!" Oops, he hadn't meant to speak out loud.

Her eyes flew open and her muscles tightened. "What's your problem?"

"You never talk to me anymore." Had he really said that? He sounded like an old married woman. *Or man. Don't be sexist.*

"Why should I? So you can critique my behavior and complain about how stupid I am?" she demanded.

"Of course not." Resentment flared at this unfair description of his statements. "I'd merely advise and counsel you."

"Same difference." Her feet vanished from his hands. Lucky felt like the prince, caught on his knees, rejected by Cinderella.

"What happened to our truce?" He realized he'd entered dangerous territory, since their pact had required him to refrain from criticizing her. But their agreement had been specifically about Andrew. It was unreasonable of her to extend that to a blanket ban on all helpful comments.

"Don't pretend we're teammates," Zora grumped. "We agreed to collaborate to secure the Adamses' donation, and apparently we succeeded."

"There's still a week to go." Lucky was grasping at straws. But surely they could resume their camaraderie.

"I promise not to screw things up before then. Satisfied?" An unfamiliar tightness transformed her into a woman he scarcely recognized, older and more guarded.

This was what he'd been trying to prevent by steering Zora past her poor choices. Before he could assess what it meant or frame another question, the tension vanished and she was once again his peppery little friend.

"I'm off to bed." She handed him her empty glass. "Do something useful. Put this in the dishwasher."

"Not the oven?"

"Whatever." Thrusting her feet into her slippers, she padded off.

Well, at least she'd addressed him directly, Lucky mused as he carried the glass to its destination. He'd count that as a victory.

How fortunate that Lucky had the male clueless gene, Zora reflected tartly while she prepared for bed. He'd mentioned nothing was certain for another week, and at the prospect of facing another week in which she might be exposed to Vince's obnoxious behavior, she'd suffered a wave of revulsion. She'd schooled her features quickly, though, and was fairly sure Lucky hadn't noticed.

She was unclear about the precise mechanism of the donation, but she assumed the billionaire would hand over a check or sign a document when he announced his gift. After that, she doubted he'd withdraw it merely because an ultrasound tech refused to service his needs.

Wrenching her mind away from the whole awful situation, Zora climbed into bed for the night. Mercifully, maternal hormones zapped her into an instant deep sleep.

Over the next few days, the housemates did everything in their power to counter the spread of the rumors about Keely. They told others the true circumstances, including

that the charges had been dropped. They pointed to ex-
amples of the older woman's kindness, which were often
overlooked due to her downbeat personality. They also
cited Laird's unscrupulous motives, although by now he
must realize they'd never let him move into their house.

It was an uphill battle. Gossip spread madly and either
distorted Laird's account even further, or else he embel-
lished it himself. According to one version that reached
Zora, Keely had gotten off murder charges on a techni-
cality. By another, she'd been suspected in the deaths of
several elderly patients. Many workers, having consulted
Laird about their personal problems in the past, were in-
clined to trust him implicitly.

Keely declined to mount a defense. "I should have
stayed home with my mom that day," she told Zora. "I
deserve my share of blame."

"Stop acting like a codependent," Zora replied, and, for
clarification, displayed the definition on her cell phone.
Keely just shrugged.

As they'd expected, Dr. Brennan supported her nurse.
Although a few of her patients who were staffers at the
medical center claimed to feel uncomfortable around Keely
due to her history, no one requested a change of doctors.

But rather than fading, the opposition was growing. In
the corridors, people avoided Keely. Zora had been ostra-
cized to an extent for stealing Stacy's husband, but it had
never sunk to this level.

Human Resources had contacted Keely and reviewed
her history, but there'd been no attempt to fire her. Nevertheless, on Thursday she informed her housemates that
she was tired of being a pariah and planned to search for
another job. Shoulders hunched, she brushed off their objections.

"She feels guilty," Karen observed after Keely left the
room. "The hardest person to forgive is yourself."

"That's ridiculous," Lucky growled. "The past is the past and we should leave it there."

Zora didn't bother to point out that he ought to leave his quarrel with his brother in the past. She was too worried about Keely to waste her energy bickering.

On Friday at lunch, a lab technician deliberately bumped Keely as she walked to their table. Fortunately, Keely kept a tight grip on her tray. Her stoic air didn't fool Zora, though. She knew her friend was close to tears.

"Don't you dare leave without eating," she told the nurse, and walked beside her to their seats. Karen, Rod and Lucky closed ranks with them.

Once they were settled, Zora dared to hope they could eat in peace. Then a tall woman of about fifty, with short brown hair and weathered skin, stalked over and stood over Keely, scowling until the chatter quieted.

"What's on your mind, Orla?" Rod demanded.

The name prodded Zora's memory. Orla Baker was a circulating nurse, which explained how Rod knew her—circulating nurses set up the operating room and checked the stock of instruments and disposable items, which they refreshed during the procedure. They played a key role in protecting patients from mistakes by verifying their identities and reviewing the site and nature of the operation with the surgeon.

"It's disgusting that she left her mother to die." She spat out the words as if it had been *her* mother who'd perished. "The DA may not have charged her, but what kind of person does that? She should be ashamed."

In the stillness, Zora spotted Laird leaning against a wall, arms folded and a smile playing around his mouth. If she'd had a rubber band, she'd have shot it at him to wipe the smirk off his face.

Rising, Lucky pointed at the psychologist. "Orla, *you* should be ashamed for allowing that man to manipulate you into bullying her. He's trying to drive her away because of petty resentment."

Zora had never admired anyone more in her life. Awkwardly, she rose, too. "Laird Maclaine played a mean prank on Keely by letting the air out of her tires. What is this, high school?" Her voice rang out with a touch of shrillness. "He also hired a detective to dig up dirt that he then distorted for his smear campaign. How can any decent person be a party to that?"

Karen sprang up. "Keely may not be slick and persuasive, but she has a kind heart and I'm with her one hundred percent."

Rod stood beside her. "That goes double for me, Orla."

The circulating nurse wavered. "My mother has Alzheimer's. I understand the stresses involved, but there's no excuse for abandoning her mother."

Keely sat silent, unwilling to speak on her own behalf. Zora feared others would take that as an indication of guilt.

Across the cafeteria, a six-foot-tall woman with a commanding air uncoiled. All attention fixed on Dr. Paige Brennan, whose eyes flashed with anger.

"This situation has been discussed at the highest levels and the case is closed," she declared. "If anyone continues creating a hostile work environment for my nurse, I will ensure that disciplinary measures are taken against them. And that is the last I or any of us had better hear about this."

The other obstetricians at her table burst into applause. With a spurt of amusement, Zora registered that the loudest clapping came from Dr. Tartikoff. Apparently he'd forgiven Keely for their long-ago dispute, or else he had zero tolerance for bullying.

Orla spoke directly to Keely. "I apologize. I shouldn't have listened to gossip."

"Have a seat." Karen waved her over. "I'm sorry about your mom, Orla. How're you holding up?"

After a brief hesitation, the circulating nurse sank into a chair. "Some days are better than others."

As the conversation flowed, Zora noted that Dr. Brennan's declaration had restored the color to Keely's face. Orla's apology appeared to have helped, too.

But best of all was watching Laird slink from the cafeteria. Paige Brennan's scorching setdown must have impressed on him that his campaign against Keely had not only failed, it had also damaged his own reputation with the top staff.

A wise person would take a long, hard look in the mirror. She didn't credit Laird with wisdom, however.

That night, Casa Wiggins celebrated the victory with meatless burgers and fizzy apple juice. There was no more talk of Keely changing jobs.

Still, it was too soon to let all her anxiety go. In less than a week, the future of the men's program would be secure, Zora hoped, and prayed silently for nothing to go wrong.

Chapter Fourteen

"I produced fifteen eggs?" From the examining table, Portia stared in dismay at Dr. Brennan. "You must be kidding!"

"That's an excellent number to ripen," the doctor assured her as Zora carefully adjusted the position of her ultrasound wand. "We'll select those in the best condition, fertilize them and choose the healthiest embryos to implant. If we have more than three, we can freeze the rest for later."

"Three? Surely two is plenty!" Portia's fingers curled, as if she longed for someone to hold her hand. Vince, who'd positioned himself in front of the ultrasound monitor, didn't appear to notice.

He'd barely glanced at Zora, either. She'd been disturbed on discovering she'd been assigned to Portia, but the scheduler had insisted.

"I'd prefer four," Vince announced. His wife gasped. Zora might not like her, but she empathized with the woman.

"That would violate hospital policy," Dr. Brennan said. "Portia, if you don't want more than two, we'll respect your wishes."

After a tense pause, the patient said, "Three will be fine."

"You're sure?"

Vince blew out an impatient breath.

Tautly, Portia said, "Yes."

Dr. Brennan jotted a note in the computer. To Zora, the doctor appeared concerned, but didn't press the point. "Now that the eggs are mature, timing is crucial. As I explained, you'll need an injection of HCG—human chorionic gonadotropin—to prepare for ovulation. Harvesting should take place thirty-six hours later."

As Zora finished her work, she half listened to the details. Normally, the patient's husband, after being shown how to give the shots, would have injected her with hormones for the past week or so, and would administer HCG at ten o'clock tonight. Instead, the Adamses had hired a visiting nurse.

"We'll set the egg retrieval for Wednesday morning," Dr. Brennan continued. "Mr. Adams, we'll coordinate with Dr. Rattigan to be sure he collects your sperm before then."

"I can attend the egg harvesting, I presume." The billionaire shifted from one foot to the other as if cramped by the confines of the examining room.

"Absolutely," the doctor said.

"We'll use the same sonographer, as per my instructions?"

Zora's stomach tightened. Today's assignment hadn't been by chance. Did the billionaire simply enjoy throwing his weight around or was there more to it?

Dr. Brennan looked startled. "The egg retrieval is a specialized procedure. We'll have a team in place."

"It's good luck to have a pregnant woman nearby. Maternal hormones and all that." Vince gestured toward Zora. "The process has gone smoothly so far with her present, hasn't it, Doctor?"

If Portia had had a death ray, Zora didn't doubt she'd have used it. *On me.*

"That's true." Dr. Brennan smiled. "However, I'm not sure we can credit Zora's maternal hormones." Without further comment about the sonographer request, she provided them directions to the hospital's retrieval room on the second floor, where the procedure would take place. "Don't eat or drink anything after midnight Tuesday, Mrs. Adams, and be sure to arrive an hour early."

"I'll be asleep for it, I hope," Portia grumbled as she sat up, finally receiving her husband's hand in assistance.

"You'll be sedated, and in recovery for two to three hours afterward," the doctor said. "We'll let you know later the same day how many eggs were retrieved. They'll be examined by an embryologist, and by Thursday we'll inform you of how many we were able to fertilize."

Thursday was the day of the press conference. Of course, the embryos wouldn't be implanted into Portia's womb for a few more days to give them time to grow in the lab. Was Vince also going to demand that Zora be present for the implantation?

He wasn't likely to succeed; as Dr. Brennan had indicated, the fertility team worked with its own techs. However, to be sure of preventing any further contact with the man, Zora could schedule her maternity leave. She had to admit that, with her ankles swollen and her abdomen sore, she was overdue.

When Keely entered the room, Zora rolled out her cart. Her knees weak with relief at having weathered the encounter with Vince, she headed around a corner toward the storage closet.

She'd just stowed the equipment when heavy male footsteps jolted her pulse into high gear. Turning, she spotted Vince Adams at a bend in the hall.

This late in the afternoon, there was no one else in view. Before she could exit, the heavyset man blocked her escape.

"What're you doing?" Zora demanded.

"You should have called me." He reached for the nearest door and shoved it open to reveal an empty examining room. "Let's talk inside."

"I'm fine right here." The words emerged breathlessly.

"This is a private conversation."

"Forget it." Zora tried to dodge past, lost her balance and stumbled. He caught her arm as if to assist, but instead pulled her into the room.

"Listen, I'm donating twenty million dollars to this hospital. And I'll spend money on you, too, if you make it worth my while." This close, she caught the scent of alcohol on his breath. Zora knew all too well what effect that had on the wrong kind of man.

"Leave me alone." She pressed her palms against his chest, but that only seemed to amuse him.

"Be nice to me, honey," he slurred.

She flashed on stories she'd heard about Vince's past: that he'd gotten his start through gang connections in a rough part of Phoenix and that a former business rival had disappeared under mysterious circumstances. Yet she'd never imagined he'd dare to assault her.

The door flew open. There stood Keely, aghast. "What is this?"

Vince glanced over his shoulder. "If you know what's good for you, Nurse, you'll keep your mouth shut."

Instead, Keely commanded, "Get your hands off her!"

"Shut up, you…"

While he was distracted, Zora grabbed a pair of scissors from a drawer. "Let go of me!"

Startled, the hulking man released her. "Neither of you says a word to anyone or you're both out of a job."

Angry breathing filled the room. No one spoke, and finally, he left. Heart pounding, Zora clutched the scissors, ready to fight if he returned.

"Are you all right?" Keely asked.

The adrenaline seeping out of her, Zora set the instrument on the counter. "Thank goodness you showed up."

How far would that monster have gone?

"Has he done anything like this before?"

It was on the tip of her tongue to deny it. *Keep the secret, don't cause problems.* But Zora had kept his secret once, and this was where it had led. "Yes, although it wasn't this bad."

"We have to report him."

Despite her outrage, Zora hesitated. "If we raise a fuss, there goes the donation. Think what that will do to the hospital, and to Lucky."

"Men like Vince Adams depend on their victims keeping silent," Keely growled. "That's how they get away with it."

"I don't want to involve the police." Zora had no idea how this situation would appear to an officer.

"You might have to," Keely said. "But you can start with Dr. Rayburn if you prefer. I'll come with you."

How brave of her, and what a great friend. Tearfully, Zora nodded. "Okay."

"First, let's settle your nerves," the nurse advised. "How about tea and peanut-butter crackers?"

"Thanks."

Twenty minutes later, after a snack in the lounge, Zora could speak without trembling. Her brain still skipped from objection to objection, however. What if her complaint smashed Lucky's dreams? What if the administrators believed she'd encouraged Vince? But she had to do this, for other potential victims as much as for herself.

It was nearly five o'clock when they reached the hospital's fifth floor. What if Dr. Rayburn had left for the day? If Zora had to wait until tomorrow, she wouldn't be able to sleep.

As they approached the executive suite, she heard movement inside. Then the last two people on earth she'd expected to see emerged into the corridor.

Vince and Portia Adams. He regarded Zora with a superior smirk. His wife gave a start, her face pale.

With the sensation of falling into an abyss, Zora realized that her tormenter had performed an end run around
her. Whatever story he'd concocted, it would make her
sound like a liar—and possibly end her career.

LUCKY KNEW SOMETHING was wrong when Keely texted
that she'd drive Zora home instead of him. Why the last-
minute change? Keely had added that she was calling a
house meeting as soon as everyone arrived.

When he tried to call Zora, her phone went to voice
mail. Was she in labor? But if she was, why would Keely
be bringing her home?

Perhaps Laird had pulled another stunt and the women
wanted to talk about it in private. Or maybe Dr. Brennan
had discovered something worrisome about Zora's pregnancy.

Adrenaline pounded through Lucky's system. If Zora
was in danger, he should be there to protect her.

In the garage, he cruised up along the ramp in search
of Keely's car. With most of the staff gone and few out-
patients or visitors on hand, he should have been able to
spot it, but no luck.

Cursing himself for wasting time, Lucky headed home.
He had to fight the tendency to stomp on the gas pedal.

Why was he reacting so strongly? It was silly and use-
less. But he kept imagining Zora's emotions in turmoil
and longing to reassure her.

At the house, he was glad when he spotted Keely's car
in the driveway. Just ahead of him, Karen pulled into the
remaining open spot, with Rod beside her.

Lucky parked at the curb and broke into a lope. "What
gives?" he asked when he came within earshot.

"No idea." Karen straightened her blazer. "I haven't
heard any gossip from our receptionist." That young

woman, Caroline Carter, reputedly had the keenest radar in the hospital.

Rod's fedora shadowed his face as the three of them followed the walkway. "I haven't picked up anything in the doctors' lounge, either."

Inside, Lucky barreled into the den, grateful that neither Karen nor Rod objected when he bypassed them. He felt a spurt of relief when he saw Zora in her usual chair, sipping a cup of juice. Keely paced nearby, unable to contain her restlessness.

Just like me. "Are you okay?" Lucky demanded.

Zora didn't answer.

"Sit down." No sign of Keely's customary reticence. "Everyone."

He took his favorite chair, while Karen and Rod slid onto the couch, not bothering to remove their shoes or hats or jackets. "Don't keep us in suspense," Rod said.

"This afternoon, I walked in on Vince Adams assaulting Zora." Disgust emphasized the deep lines in Keely's face.

"He did what?" Lucky sprang up, prepared to find the man and pummel him. "Were you hurt? You should go to the police."

"Let us finish, please." When he subsided, Keely described the scene she'd interrupted in an examining room. Thank goodness she'd arrived when she had, although Lucky would have paid a fair amount of money to watch Zora stab that jerk with scissors.

But before they could take the matter to Dr. Rayburn, Vince had beaten them to the punch, claiming Zora had tried to extort money by threatening to accuse him of harassing her.

"Mark can't believe that," Karen protested when Keely paused for breath. "It's ridiculous."

"Still, I'm glad to have Keely as a witness." Zora's voice trembled. "And I showed Dr. Rayburn the business card

Vince gave me with his private number scrawled on the back. He pressed it on me the last time he cornered me."

"He's done this before?" The revelation sickened Lucky. "Why didn't you report it?"

"It didn't go this far," she told him. "And I was worried it might have an impact on the men's program."

"The program isn't your responsibility," Karen said.

"But I care about—about the rest of the staff," Zora replied.

"You were protecting me?" Lucky would never allow her to put her safety at risk. "I didn't ask you to do that."

"You were happy enough when Portia agreed to in vitro," Zora shot back. "He all but said he'd leave her for some 'earth mother,' as he described me, if she didn't agree to in vitro instead of insisting on surrogacy."

Stunned, Lucky recalled the scene outside Dr. Rattigan's examining room. He'd never known the details of how Portia had made her decision. And all this while, she'd kept Vince's mistreatment a secret?

Once, long ago, Lucky had vowed never again to let down anyone he loved the way he'd let down his parents. Yet now he had. Worse, by scheduling Zora to work that first morning because he valued her insight, he'd put her in harm's way.

Wordlessly, he listened as the conversation moved on around him. In the administrator's office, Mark had been accompanied by attorney Tony Franco. They'd assured Zora that her job was safe and that she had every right to contact the police.

"Great idea." Lucky would love to see Vince hauled off in handcuffs.

"As if I'd have any chance against a billionaire and his legal team," Zora said miserably.

"We have honest cops in Safe Harbor," Karen responded. "Tony Franco's brother is a police detective."

"Vince will just repeat his claim that I tried to extort

money from him," Zora said. "How can I prove I didn't? And if he sues me for slander, I can't afford to fight."

It was unfair that his wealth enabled a man like Vince to crush people, as he'd already done with Rod. If only Lucky had been the one to discover that scene today, he'd have taught the bastard a lesson on the spot.

And probably lost his job, not to mention being locked up for assault. But it would have felt good to smash his fists into the man's oily face.

"Dr. Rayburn seemed worried about the emotional and physical effects on Zora," Keely put in. "He offered her an extra two months of paid maternity leave, not in lieu of anything else, just for health reasons."

"He suggested I go on leave immediately while he sorts this out," Zora added. "I refuse to slink away as if I did anything wrong, but I am going to start my leave on Monday, because I already had that in mind."

"Extra paid leave—that's a positive thing, anyway," Karen said.

"How does Dr. Rayburn intend to sort this out?" Lucky persisted. Zora had been attacked at work, and other staffers could be at risk, too. If only Vince weren't so rich, and the hospital staff so eager for his donation.

Including me. It revolted Lucky to think of how hard he'd worked to keep Vince involved with Safe Harbor.

"Dr. Rayburn said there are complicating issues." Having practically worn a path in the carpet with her pacing, Keely plopped into an armchair.

"Like what? Vince's money?" Rod grumbled.

"He and Portia are patients, so disrupting their care would be unethical if no wrongdoing is proved." Zora clasped her hands atop her baby bump. "It's a crucial week for them."

"The hospital should cancel that damn press conference." No matter what the donation meant for Lucky or his doctor, he'd never sacrifice an innocent person's well-being. Especially Zora's.

"Dr. Rayburn has to discuss it with the hospital corporation," Keely said. "They'll make the final decision. Except he was very clear that he will not allow any repercussions against Zora or me."

"Dr. Brennan would be up in arms if he did, I'm sure," Karen said.

"Along with the rest of the medical staff," Rod added. "No one would believe Vince's story."

Zora set her empty cup on the table. "Keely and I aren't exactly the most popular members of the staff."

"You've seen what our household can do," Lucky reminded her. "If you need us, we're here."

Both women nodded. "Oh, we aren't supposed to discuss this," Zora added. "Please don't tell anyone else."

Despite an eagerness to rally the troops behind Zora, Lucky supposed he had to respect her decision. "All right." *For now.*

"How about dinner?" Karen got to her feet. "I'll bet the mommy-to-be is starving."

Rod stood also. "My cooking skills may be notoriously bad, but Jack taught me how to cook angel-hair pasta with wine and onions. It doesn't take long. And the alcohol in the wine evaporates."

"I'll fix a salad," Lucky volunteered.

The dinner went well, but he continued to be frustrated for the rest of the evening. He should be the person Zora turned to, but instead she remained glued to Keely's side. Lucky tried in vain to catch her alone so he could massage her tense little shoulders. Or fetch her ice cream— why didn't she send him on errands anymore?

How ironic that he'd criticized her for leading a messy life. Now she'd landed in her biggest crisis yet, and the person most to blame—after Vince, of course—was Lucky himself.

Yet again, he'd been responsible for causing pain to someone he cared about. And yet again, there didn't seem to be any way to make up for his mistakes.

Chapter Fifteen

Catching sweet, sympathetic glances from Lucky all evening, Zora yearned to fly to him. Temporary though the respite might be, she longed to curl up in his arms and enjoy the illusion of safety.

But it *was* an illusion. She understood Lucky too well. Their relationship could only progress to a certain point before he'd slam the door on her. She and her babies would never fit his requirements for a perfect family.

How ironic that, while she failed to measure up to Lucky's standards, his influence had helped her shake free of her old codependent habits. She'd told off Andrew, stood up to Vince Adams and marched into Dr. Rayburn's office when her instincts screamed at her to flee.

It had been terrifying to confront two such powerful men in the meeting. Dr. Rayburn had towered over her dauntingly when they'd shaken hands. As for Tony Franco, beneath his reserved manner lurked a brain capable of raising who-knew-what legal complications against which an ordinary mortal was defenseless.

Zora had been grateful that Keely was there, and for the strength that she was beginning to realize had been within her all along. She'd managed not to break down in tears when the administrator repeated the lie Vince had told them. She'd stuck doggedly to the facts, painful as they were. There'd been two previous incidents, and she had the business card to prove it. Not much evidence, but it helped, as did Keely's testimony.

Tossing and turning in bed that night, she searched without success for a solution. If the Adamses canceled their planned donation, the whole hospital would suffer and Lucky might have to go elsewhere to build his career. But if the grant went forward, how could Zora stay? The vengeful billionaire would find a way to destroy her.

In the morning, she received a message from her sister: Got the job! Start in 3 weeks!

Under other circumstances, that would have been fantastic news. Now, Zora worried that if Vince saw her identical twin, he'd target Zady, too.

She arrived at the medical center on Tuesday with her senses on high alert. As the day progressed, no one mentioned Vince's accusations, but the news spread about Zora starting maternity leave on Monday. The hospital's public relations director, Jennifer Serra Martin, presented Zora with a pair of adorable teddy bears that played lullabies. Dr. T's nurse, Ned Norwalk, slipped Zora a gift card to Kitchens, Cooks and Linens.

"I'm not sure whether you're short of pots and pans, but you can always use more knives." He whisked off before she could ask what he meant. Had that been a veiled reference to her scissors wielding?

By Tuesday's end, the press conference hadn't been canceled, nor, apparently, had the next day's egg retrieval. And she learned that Vince had undergone the procedure to collect his sperm. The only change Zora observed was that the billionaire was now accompanied everywhere by a male patient care coordinator, supposedly to ensure his comfort.

And to protect me and the other women on staff?

On Wednesday morning, Zora was again assigned to Dr. Brennan's patients. No danger of running into the Adamses, whose egg retrieval was taking place in the hospital. Dr. Brennan, Zora discovered, had arranged for Dr. Zack Sargent to perform the procedure on the grounds that he performed more of them.

The moment she spotted Zora, Dr. Brennan zeroed in on her. "I'm sorry that you were assaulted."

"I'm fine."

"It was an unforgivable act, and I'm furious that it took place on my watch," the tall woman said. "If you need me to go to bat for you, just say the word."

Zora thanked her, pleased to have another person on her side.

At lunch, aware of prying ears, Zora and her housemates were careful not to discuss what was foremost on everyone's minds. She had almost finished eating when a call came from Dr. Rayburn's assistant, asking Zora to meet with him.

"I'll go with you," Keely announced.

"You have patients," Lucky reminded her.

"You can't let them down," Zora echoed. Despite her words, Zora shivered to think of what lay ahead. What if the corporation insisted on firing her? What if… Her brain wouldn't stretch further than that.

"Dr. Rattigan's in surgery for another hour, so I'll go with you." Lucky piled her dishes onto his tray. "No arguments."

"I didn't plan to raise any."

On the elevator ride to the fifth floor, Zora held Lucky's hand. Tension rippled across the muscles in his neck and arms, with the ironic effect that the dragon protruding from beneath his navy blue sleeve appeared to be winking at her.

"I hope I don't break down." She released her grip as they stepped into the empty hallway. "I've always been terrified that someday everything would fall apart and I'd be alone."

He touched her shoulder gently. "You aren't alone."

Zora blinked back tears. Impulsively, she asked, "What's *your* biggest fear?"

"Failing the people I love," Lucky said without hesitation. "And I'm not about to do that again."

Did he include her among the people he loved? Zora cautioned herself against leaping to conclusions. She had a bad habit of hearing only what she wished to hear.

"Don't go out on a limb for my sake," she told him.

"My integrity isn't for sale," Lucky answered. "Cole's isn't, either. He has opportunities elsewhere, although before he leaves Safe Harbor, I'm sure he'll consider the impact on Stacy."

"Oh, great." Zora hadn't considered how wide the fallout might be from the loss of Vince's donation. "As if I haven't done Stacy enough harm already."

"You did her a favor, taking Andrew away," Lucky returned. "I should have realized that sooner."

In the administrative suite, the assistant regarded Lucky in surprise. "I'm here for moral support," he said.

"Hold on." She picked up her phone.

From one of several inner rooms, Tony Franco appeared, his rust-brown hair rumpled as if he'd been running his fingers through it. After introducing himself to Lucky, he shook hands with them both. "Dr. Rayburn and I would like to speak to Mrs. Raditch alone."

"Without her lawyer?" Lucky demanded.

Tony gave a start. "If she wishes…"

"Lucky, that isn't necessary." How could she afford it? Also, since Edmond worked as a consultant for the hospital, he had a conflict of interest. Where would she find another lawyer on short notice?

"Then I'm sitting in," Lucky responded firmly. "I'll keep quiet, I promise."

To Zora's surprise, the attorney acquiesced. "Very well."

Tony's expression remained opaque. Did they learn

how to do that in law school? she wondered, and pictured a classroom full of law students training their features to remain flat.

When they entered Dr. Rayburn's office, the administrator rose to shake their hands, and it was obvious he hadn't mastered the same art. In his face, she read unease, a touch of surprise at Lucky's presence and regret.

Oh, damn.

True to his statement, Lucky took a seat in a corner of the large office. Dr. Rayburn, whom she'd expected to retreat behind the desk, instead positioned himself in a chair beside hers. "I'll get straight to the point. The corporation insists we accept the Adamses' sponsorship of the men's program and move forward with tomorrow's press conference."

Zora swallowed. She hadn't seriously expected the hospital to reject millions of dollars simply to spare the feelings of one ultrasound tech, had she?

"They would have preferred that I not talk to you directly about this, but that's bull," he continued.

"Mark," the attorney warned.

"Hey, Tony, you're the guy who recommends our doctors apologize to patients when they've made a mistake." Dr. Rayburn's thick eyebrows rose in emphasis. "Isn't it your opinion that honesty and contrition cut the risk of lawsuits?"

"Mark!" Tony said more forcefully. The reference to lawsuits must have set off alarm bells in the man's head.

Dr. Rayburn returned his attention to Zora. "I disagree with this decision, but I've done all I can. I've negotiated for you to receive six months of paid parental leave." Normally, staffers received two months. "Afterward, you can resume your job if you wish, with a guarantee that you won't be assigned to attend to either of the Adamses."

Relief warred with an awareness of how touchy the

situation would be, in numerous respects. "What about my sister?"

"Your sister?" Dr. Rayburn asked blankly.

"My identical twin sister is joining the staff." *Please don't let this mess things up for Zady.* "She'll be assisting the new urologist, Dr. Davis."

The administrator regarded the attorney, who fielded the question. "That's tricky, since Mr. Adams is a patient in the men's program. However, we can take precautions so she won't be put at risk."

But what about other women who might be subjected to Vince? Then Zora remembered the patient care coordinator shadowing the billionaire. Apparently, safeguards were already in place. "Okay."

"To bring you up to date, the corporate vice president will be flying in for tomorrow's events," Dr. Rayburn said. "There'll be a gala reception beforehand at the yacht club. The press conference will be at 5:00 p.m. in the auditorium. The staff is invited."

"I plan to skip it." Zora had no interest in watching the billionaire gloat.

"That's your choice." Dr. Rayburn still sounded dissatisfied. "You've undergone a traumatic experience. The hospital will be happy to provide sessions with a therapist."

With Laird? Zora's fists clenched. "No, thanks."

"We can arrange outside counseling with a woman." Tony must have noticed her reaction.

"I don't think that will be necessary. But I'll let you know if I change my mind." Despite her anxiety, Zora hadn't suffered nightmares about the incident. Still, she respected the value of professional help. If she'd received it during her divorce, she might not have clung to her foolish delusions for so long.

Neither she nor Lucky had any more questions, and the meeting ended. She still disliked the situation, but not enough to consider leaving Safe Harbor.

In the hall, Lucky kept pace with her. "Are you okay? I'm glad you mentioned Zady. I was wondering whether to bring her up, but you beat me to it."

"I appreciate the backup," she said. "Having someone who was in my corner there was important."

How had she failed for so long to realize what a strong, kind man he was? Of course, his previous antagonism toward her might have had something to do with that, Zora reflected.

And now? Circumstances had thrown them onto the same team, their loyalties more or less aligned. But was she really destined to remain nothing more than friends with him?

Now that she'd summoned the courage to confront her problems, maybe she ought to call Lucky to task for ignoring how much they meant to each other. But standing up for herself at work was one thing. Relationships were an entirely different matter. Where men were concerned, Zora still didn't trust her instincts.

That afternoon, the gossip mill at the hospital focused on possible developments at tomorrow's press conference, and she heard no mention of Vince's misconduct. On the drive home, Lucky agreed with Zora's observations.

"Dr. Rattigan doesn't seem to have any idea what happened between you and that jerk or that there was any question about accepting the donation," he told her as they headed south. "He was singing to himself in French this afternoon, which means he's excited."

"Why in French?" Zora asked.

"His father's French," Lucky said. "They aren't close, but Cole has an affinity for the language."

"At least he's happy." She sighed. "And this means he and Stacy won't have to consider moving." *Nor you, either.*

"I only wish the circumstances were different." Stopped at a red light, Lucky drummed his hands on the wheel.

"When I threw myself into winning Vince's support for the program, I had no idea he'd harm someone I care about."

"Even me?" Zora teased.

"Especially you!" But his next words disappointed her. "Or anyone." The light changed and he tapped the gas pedal. "If the men's program does expand and I land a management post, I'll stand by my nurses. That man better leave them alone."

"After he donates the money, surely he won't continue meddling." Zora assumed that was the case. "If he and Portia have children, there'll be no reason for further treatment."

"I suspect he'll find a way to keep us dancing on his strings." Lucky's jaw tightened.

Reluctantly, Zora agreed. Then she decided not to worry about matters beyond her control. For once, her practice in denial stood her in good stead.

A LOT OF stomping shook the two-story house that night. Rod stomped to and from the kitchen, complaining about the upbeat conversations he'd overheard in the operating room. "Everyone thinks Vince's generosity is fantastic. Don't they realize they're bringing in a monster?"

Lucky did his share of stomping as he carted a pair of cribs upstairs and assembled them in Zora's oversize closet-turned-nursery, which had a small window. To accommodate her displaced clothes, he also hauled a rack to the second-floor alcove.

While he was happy to help, he mused that Andrew ought to be chipping in so the new mom could afford the larger downstairs suite. Fond as Lucky was of his quarters, he would willingly swap.

Did Zora plan to let her ex continue to ignore his financial obligations? Surely she didn't maintain the fantasy that he'd return to her after the babies' birth. Yet in spite of everything, she might.

Lucky feared that in her mind, the twins would always be Andrew's babies. And with his current marriage dissolving, the man might decide to toy with her emotions again, just to feed his ego. Until he found another wide-eyed young woman to fall for his manipulations, and broke Zora's heart all over again.

Lucky went downstairs for a snack. "You going to the press conference tomorrow?" he asked Rod, who'd taken the next-to-last slice of apple pie left over from dinner.

"You bet. I never miss a chance to see my girls." The slender man tugged at his short beard, which, like his hair, was going gray. Rod was only in his early forties, but stress from his long custody battle might have played a role in giving him more gray hairs. "I'm sure he'll require Tiff and Amber to show up, since it's scheduled after school hours."

"I'm not sure I should attend," Lucky admitted. "My opinion of Vince might show on my face."

"I doubt he'll care," Rod said.

In the den, a phone rang. Lucky heard Karen answer. "Edmond? What…?" Then her tone grew urgent. "Of course. I'll meet you at the hospital. No problem!"

Lucky's brain leaped to the likeliest conclusion: Melissa was having her triplets. In their haste to talk to Karen, he and Rod collided in the doorway. "Sorry!"

"Ow, damn it!" Rod snapped. "I mean, I'm sorry, too."

"Anyone need medical attention?" Karen inquired dryly. "No? Great. Rod, want to ride with me to pick up Dawn? She's spending the night with us." Karen occasionally babysat the seven-year-old, who always proved good company.

"Sure." Rod plucked his fedora from a coat rack. "Melissa's in labor?"

"Her water broke. She's at thirty weeks, earlier than they were hoping for but not bad for a multiple birth. They're assembling a team."

"I'll notify Zora and Keely." There were others who should be informed, too, Lucky thought. "Also Anya and Jack. Should I make up one of the couches for Dawn?"

"She can sleep with me," Karen assured him.

Rod sighed. "Guess I'm alone in my bed tonight."

She punched his arm. "Discretion!"

He grinned.

"Please tell Melissa and Edmond I'm rooting for them," Lucky said. Despite the skill of the hospital's doctors and nurses, the birth of triplets would pose a challenge.

"I will." Karen headed out with Rod behind her.

If all went well, this would be a joyous event, Lucky reflected on his way upstairs to spread the news. What a timely reminder of the miracles wrought at Safe Harbor.

Although his gut churned at the prospect of tomorrow's press conference, the donation would enable the staff to perform even more miracles. Too bad the price tag included putting up with a preening, triumphant Vince Adams. At Zora's expense.

Chapter Sixteen

"We had a devil of a time agreeing on names for three girls," Edmond remarked to Zora at midday as they viewed the triplets in the intermediate care nursery.

Weighing over three pounds and with mature lungs, little Simone, Jamie and Lily were in excellent shape. Nevertheless, they had to be observed for signs of infection or other potential problems.

Wrapped in pink and attached to monitors, the trio were adorable. Zora's arms ached to reach through the viewing window and hold them. A tiny yawn from one—was that Jamie?—was almost too cute to be real.

"I still don't have a name for my son." Zora rested her hand on her by-now enormous bulge. "My daughter's name will be Elizabeth."

"After her grandmother?" The attorney knew Betsy, of course.

She nodded. "I read that the first Queen Elizabeth was named after *her* grandmother."

"Here's a bit of trivia—both her grandmothers were called Elizabeth." Edmond adjusted his glasses.

"I'm impressed that you know that."

"History fascinates me. Melissa and I used to travel and tour historic sites as often as we could." He gazed dreamily at the babies. "Someday we'll take the kids abroad."

"I'm envious." Since there was no one else nearby, Zora added, "Any further word from my charming ex?"

"His attorney indicated he'll comply with the law," Edmond said. "I did forward your list of expenses, but I've heard nothing since."

"Thanks, and I'm sorry to bring this up when you must be exhausted." Zora had spoken without thinking.

"I took a nap this morning." The new father grinned. "I went home and crashed after dropping Dawn at school." The excited seven-year-old had visited the hospital early to meet her new cousins, after spending the night with Karen.

"You've adjusted well to fatherhood." As Melissa's former housemate, Zora recalled that her friend's marriage had broken up over Edmond's refusal to have children.

"I'm grateful for the second chance. I had no idea what I was missing." Joy shone from his face.

A lot of events had changed Edmond, from accepting custody of his niece after his sister went to prison for robbery to the discovery that Melissa had "adopted" three embryos. Parenting Dawn had awakened Edmond's suppressed instincts, and his renewed love for his once and future wife had filled in the rest.

Once, Zora had believed Andrew might undergo a similar change of heart. Witnessing his cruelty to Lin had erased the last of her delusions, however. That, and being around Lucky. He demonstrated how a man ought to behave, in contrast to her father, her stepfather and her ex-husband.

A touch of heartburn roused Zora with a reminder that she ought to eat. "I'm going to the cafeteria," she told Edmond. "Please assure Melissa I'll visit her later."

"I'll do that," he said. "And soon she'll be visiting you in the maternity ward, too."

"That's true, isn't it?" When Lucky installed the cribs last night, it had emphasized to Zora that soon her babies would emerge into the world. Despite an eagerness to lighten her physical load, she wasn't sure she was ready to cope. But then, what single mother *was* ready to cope with twins?

On the ground floor, receptionist Caroline Carter waved her to a halt. "I have something for you. Can you hang on a minute?"

"Sure."

The young woman darted into her nearby office, returning with a children's book. "Sorry it's not wrapped, but I wanted to catch you before your leave starts."

"How beautiful!" Zora traced a finger over the stunning cover photograph of a butterfly. The book described how to study nature in your backyard, a topic she found especially relevant in view of the fact that her home was located next to an estuary.

"Nurse Harper Gladstone took the photos," Caroline said. "And her husband wrote the text."

Harper, a widow with a young daughter, had married a biology teacher. "It's perfect. Thank you."

"Enjoy your lunch. Oh!" With a confidential air, Caroline leaned closer, her brown eyes alight with her favorite subject: gossip. "Did you hear that Vince Adams assaulted a woman?"

Zora couldn't breathe. Apparently, the news had spread. Yet Caroline didn't seem to realize she was addressing the target of that assault. "Who told you that?"

"Laird," the receptionist said.

Since he had an office near Dr. Rayburn's, he must have caught wind of the confidential discussions. What a creep to shoot his mouth off! "He isn't always truthful." That was the best Zora could do.

"Yes, but he usually has reliable sources." Caroline shrugged. "Do you suppose it will spoil the press conference?"

"The less we talk about it, the better." Zora hoped the other woman would heed her warning.

"You're right." Caroline wrinkled her nose. "I keep swearing I'm going to stop spreading rumors. It's addictive, though."

"Thanks for the book. I'm sure the twins and I will enjoy it." On that note, Zora beelined for the cafeteria.

If word of what Vince had done reached the media, how would that affect the billionaire's donation? And if her name became attached to the rumor, there was no predicting what the reporters would say. The notion of the press camping out on Karen's lawn horrified her. Whiffs of swamp gas might discourage them, but she doubted it.

Zora decided not to mention the story to her friends. As she'd said to Caroline, the more discreet they were, the less risk the press conference would be disrupted.

THE STAFF, REPORTERS and VIPs filled the auditorium, leaving Lucky and a scattering of press to line the edges. Standing in the back above the steeply raked rows, he studied the scene uneasily.

Seated on the stage with the administrator, the public relations director, the corporate vice president and the Adamses, Cole appeared relaxed and cheerful. He evidently didn't notice what Lucky considered warning signs that something was going to go wrong.

Vince's ruddy complexion was flushed and, judging by his gait when mounting the steps, he'd imbibed more than he should have at the reception. While he sprawled on his chair with his legs apart, Portia's shoulders were painfully stiff beneath her ivory suit jacket. Her gaze traveled frequently to her daughters, who fidgeted in the front row beside their grandmother.

Around Lucky, more members of the press squeezed in, with cameras bearing the logos of LA news teams and a couple of national networks. He hadn't seen this much media since Cole presented a speech on men's declining sperm rates, sparking a furor that had blown the matter wildly out of proportion. Surely Dr. Rattigan's involvement couldn't account for this much interest, but what did?

Next to him, a reporter murmured to a photographer, "Wonder if Adams can keep his hands to himself on stage? That PR lady's awfully pretty."

"And he's well oiled," the other man responded. "Hey, it's a slow news day. We can always hope."

Anxiety churned in Lucky's stomach. What had these guys heard? He was grateful that Keely had driven Zora home earlier, sparing her any immediate fallout.

On the stage, Jennifer Martin took the microphone. After a brief greeting, she introduced Medical Center Management Vice President Chandra Yashimoto.

The dark-haired executive, whose striking black-and-white suit rivaled Portia's for elegance, glided to center stage. With a practiced smile, she sketched the history of the medical center's transformation from a community hospital to a national center for fertility and maternity care.

When she cited the importance of Dr. Cole Rattigan, Lucky braced for an audience reaction. If reporters planned to revive their silly stories terming him Dr. Baby Crisis, they'd start lobbing questions now. But no one reacted.

They seemed to be waiting. For what?

Ms. Yashimoto didn't call on Dr. Rayburn, whose furrowed brow reflected a less than enthusiastic attitude, nor did she ask Cole to speak. Instead, she cut to the announcement: Safe Harbor was poised to become an international center for the treatment of and research into men's fertility, thanks to a twenty-million-dollar gift from San Diego financier Vincent Adams and his wife, both of whom were—according to Chandra—well-known philanthropists.

Lights flashed and lenses clicked as Vince strode to the front and shook hands with the vice president. A staff photographer captured the moment, but to Lucky it seemed that others snapped only perfunctory shots.

"Thank you, Chandra." Vince beamed, in his element as the center of attention. "This program means more to me than merely putting my name on a building. It means leaving a legacy of children, mine and other men's, that will last until the end of time."

"There's modesty for you," the nearby reporter observed in a low tone.

"This week, my wife and I moved forward in our quest to expand our family," Vince continued. "My wife prefers that I not go into detail, but thanks to Dr. Rattigan, we expect to have a blessed event of our own by next year."

Portia's eyes narrowed. No doubt she'd asked him to keep that private, too, especially since they hadn't implanted the embryos yet.

The reporter murmured, "I wonder if she'll be the only woman popping out his offspring."

Was the man referring to Zora? Lucky wouldn't put it past the more irresponsible members of the press to imply that her pregnancy was the result of a liaison with Vince. Never mind facts or her DNA test—they'd drag her name through the mud.

When Vince paused for breath, a man in a central row scrambled to his feet. "Mr. Adams, this morning your former personal assistant Geneva Gabriel filed a five-million-dollar lawsuit against you in San Diego Superior Court, alleging sexual assault. We understand the district attorney is investigating. Care to comment?"

That explained the reporters' snide exchanges! Lucky experienced a spurt of relief, then immediately regretted it. He was sorry that Ms. Gabriel had suffered, too.

"She's just out for my money." Vince spluttered with fury. "I fired that witch because she's stupid and incompetent."

Chandra Yashimoto stood frozen. Cole's face registered his confusion, while Lucky could have sworn Mark Rayburn was barely suppressing a smile.

Jennifer rose to the occasion, literally. Crossing the stage to seize the microphone again, she said, "I'm sure Mr. Adams will have his attorney respond to your questions. My assistant is handing out a press release with the details of Mr. and Mrs. Adams' generous gift. Thank you for joining us."

After a few inaudible words to Vince, she steered him and Portia toward a side door. Shaking with anger, the billionaire gestured at the front row, summoning his daughters. Tiffany might have stood her ground, but when Amber raced up the steps, the older girl followed.

Cole and the others left the stage via a second exit. Unable to reach them as the crowd filled the aisles, Lucky shuffled out with the rest of the audience.

In the corridor, he passed Laird, who'd shanghaied a couple of puzzled reporters. "I'm embarrassed to be associated with a hospital that would accept money from a man like Vince Adams," the man announced. "That's why I'm handing in my notice and joining a private practice in Newport Beach. My name is Laird Maclaine."

A listener thrust out a small mic. "Are you a doctor in the men's fertility program?"

"I'm the staff psychologist."

"You're the staff opportunist," Lucky called, and dodged away. He wove through the milling assemblage, in case his doctor had been hemmed in by the press. He'd learned from experience that a show of muscle could prove handy.

Rounding a corner, he spotted a small group bunched near the staff entrance—the Adamses and the public relations director. All Lucky could see of the man blocking their escape was his fedora.

"You're in no condition to drive." Rod's voice was shrill with emotion. "The girls stay here."

"Get out of my way, Vintner." The bigger man towered over his opponent.

"Rod, you're making things worse." That was Portia, hovering beside her daughters. Jennifer, the only non-family member of the group, regarded the scene with uncertainty.

Where was Mark? The administrator, a former football player, was a physical match for Vince, but he must be occupied whisking Cole and Chandra out of harm's way.

"You're drunk," Rod persisted. "I'll take the girls to their grandmother." They'd left Helen behind in their rush, Lucky saw.

"Out of our way!" Vince shoved Rod, hard. The girls gasped as the smaller man staggered and fell against the wall. When blood spurted from his nose, Vince raised his fists in a victory gesture.

Rage surged in Lucky at the man's brutality. His fury mounted when the billionaire clamped onto Amber's wrist. "Let's go."

His younger daughter wriggled fruitlessly. "We're not supposed to get in a car with a drunk driver."

"Shut up." Vince yanked the girl toward the exit.

"Leave her alone!" Tiffany screamed.

As their stepfather wrenched open the door, Lucky barreled forward. The others parted, leaving him a clear shot at the distracted billionaire, who half turned to gape at him.

Lucky's kick hit its target: Vince's knee. With a cry of pain, the big man released Amber and stumbled out into the parking area reserved for administrators.

"Let's get out of here." Tiffany gestured to her sister. "Dad needs a doctor." Clearly, she meant Rod.

"Never mind him. You're both coming with us," their mother snapped.

"No." Tiffany slid an arm around the dazed Rod, who had a tissue pressed to his nose. "Thank you, Lucky."

"My pleasure."

Portia flinched as, outside, her husband bellowed for her. "He's too impaired to drive," Lucky warned, following her through the door. "Please stop him before he injures someone."

She glared. "Mind your own business."

"Where are the girls?" Vince roared, standing between his high-performance sports coupe and Dr. Rayburn's sedan.

"They're staying," Lucky retorted.

"I'll have you fired for this," the billionaire snarled.

"You planning to push me around, too?" Lucky demanded. "Or do you only attack people smaller than you?"

He could see Vince weighing the urge to punch him out. The man might have tried, but a shift of position put too much weight on his injured knee and he stumbled and then produced a deep groan. Regaining his balance with a hand on the sedan, the man snarled at his wife, "In the car. Now!"

"Let her drive," Lucky said. "For both your sakes."

"Shut up, you punk."

Mouth pressed into a thin line, Portia slid into the passenger seat while Vince got behind the wheel. How sad that she'd thrown in her lot with her husband, willing to sacrifice her safety to maintain her wealth and status. Worse, she'd been ready to risk her daughters' safety, too.

A hand on Lucky's arm alerted him to Jennifer's presence. Holding her phone in the other hand, she said, "Thanks for intervening. I arranged with Mark to make sure Rod gets medical treatment and the girls stay with their grandmother."

"Watch out!"

They beat a quick retreat as the sports car shot in reverse. After scraping the bumper of another car, Vince twisted the wheel, hit the gas and zoomed forward. He and Portia disappeared around the building.

"I'm calling the cops." Lucky took out his cell. "That's a hit-and-run. Also, he shouldn't be driving in his condition."

"Good." Jennifer straightened her spine. "I'd better corral the press. I don't want them harassing the staff."

Lucky thought of Laird. "Nor do we want the staff taking advantage of this mess."

Despite a puzzled glance, she didn't request an explanation. Duty was calling, and she hurried inside.

He dialed 911 and explained the situation to the dispatcher. Although Lucky hadn't observed which direction Vince took, the Adamses' beach cottage lay south of here. The most direct route would be along Pacific Coast Highway.

The dispatcher thanked him and said she'd alert patrol officers to be on the lookout. One would stop by to take a report about the hit-and-run, as well.

Bathed in October sunlight, Lucky eased his breathing. He'd never imagined such a devastating outcome of today's announcement. There was nothing anyone could have done to prevent this, he supposed. The lawsuit filing had changed everything.

Damn Vince and his arrogance. But at least the girls were safe. As for Rod's injury, the man had every right to report the assault and to sue for damages. However, he'd learned a hard lesson about the difficulties of fighting Vince in court.

Checking his phone, Lucky saw he'd missed a call from Zora. He returned it, and after two rings, her excited voice said, "Lucky! Keely's driving me to the hospital."

"Why?"

"I'm in labor!" she said happily.

"Everything's okay?"

"Yes—the pains aren't bad yet," she said. "I called ahead and they're setting up a C-section. Honestly, I was surprised what a relief it is. And the day after Melissa! Must be fate."

He gave a low chuckle. "Well, if that doesn't put the cap on an already over-the-top day."

"What happened?" She must not have been following the news. He presumed that radio reporters were already describing the brouhaha on the air.

"Vince's former assistant is suing him for sexual assault," Lucky told her. "He stalked out in a huff. Guess you're not the only one he's victimized."

"I hope she nails him to the wall."

"Five million dollars' worth of wall," he agreed.

"Yay for her." Then Zora gasped, "Watch out!"

"What…?"

The call went dead.

Inside Lucky, fear tightened into a knot. Had there been an accident? Surely not, yet…

The shortest route from Karen's house to the hospital was via Pacific Coast Highway—directly in Vince's path. His heart nearly stopped.

Don't be ridiculous.

On his phone, Lucky pressed Zora's number. He listened, struggling for calm, as it rang and rang, then went to voice mail.

He heard a siren in the distance. Then another. They sounded as if they were heading for Coast Highway.

Lucky began to pray.

Chapter Seventeen

The sports car appeared out of nowhere, weaving madly across lanes, and only Keely's swift veer to the right prevented a crash. Overcorrecting, the other car swerved, hit the curb and went airborne.

With a horrifying crunch, it landed on its roof. Shaken, Zora realized that she'd recognized the occupants as they sped past: Vince and Portia.

A siren shrilled almost instantly. Within seconds, a patrol cruiser and a fire truck swarmed in, followed by paramedics. An officer stopped behind Keely's brown sedan, which was parked on the right shoulder.

The police had been watching for Vince's car, he explained while examining Keely's license. After asking whether the two women were injured—neither was—he prepared to take their statements.

Zora cried out as another pain gripped her. "She's in labor," Keely explained.

"I'll call for another ambulance."

"We're only two miles from the hospital. It'll be faster if I drive," Keely said. "Don't worry. I'm a nurse."

After radioing the dispatcher, the officer offered to follow them in case they required aid, and they accepted. As they drove, Zora and Keely listened to a news station's account of billionaire Vince Adams facing a harassment lawsuit. There was no mention of the crash yet.

As the initial shock wore off, Zora recalled Vince's puffy face behind the windshield and Portia's terrified expression. How weird that the Adamses had nearly hit them. Since she hadn't observed any reporters in pursuit, Vince had no one but his arrogance to blame for his speeding.

However, he was probably in no condition to blame anyone. And what about Portia?

Zora regarded Keely, who'd remained stoic throughout the incident. "That was awful. Do you suppose they're…?"

"Badly injured or worse, unless they had their seat belts fastened." Swinging onto Hospital Way ahead of the cruiser, the nurse said, "I don't believe there was anyone else in the car."

The girls. How could Zora have forgotten them? "I sure hope not."

They stopped at the maternity entrance. Staffers rushed out with a gurney to assist them.

Keely checked a message on her phone. "Dr. Brennan's on site. She'll do the surgery."

"Fantastic." That was reassuring.

"They have the pediatricians prepping, too." There'd be one for each twin, the doctor had said earlier.

"Okay." After the near miss on the road, Zora had no strength left. Fortunately, she could simply lie back and entrust her care to the experts.

Her thoughts returned to the Adamses. Vince might be a repulsive man, but she'd never wished him dead. And certainly not Portia. How badly were they hurt? How would this affect their daughters?

As Zora was transferred onto the gurney, Lucky raced to her, breathing hard. "Is she okay? Zora?"

"I'm fine. Sorry I left you dangling." In the heat of the moment, she'd forgotten their interrupted conversation. Later, she'd been vaguely aware of her cell ringing, but had been too overwrought to answer.

He stared down, desperately drinking in the sight of her. She'd never seen him so shaken.

"The Adamses nearly hit us." Zora stroked his arm, yearning to take away his tormented expression. "Keely steered out of their path."

"What about Vince and Portia?"

"We saw their car flip over," Keely said, joining them after conferring with the officer. "Beyond that, I have no idea."

Lucky swept the older nurse into a hug. "Bless you!"

"I didn't sneeze," she said tartly.

"You kept a cool head, from what I hear," Lucky responded.

Keely extricated herself from the hug. "Anyone else would have done the same."

"Not necessarily." Lucky turned to Zora. "How's my sweetheart?"

"Still trembling." Lying on the gurney, Zora was glad when he took her hand, his strength flowing into her. She wished *he* was the babies' father. Then he could stay with her, comfort her and share her joy.

An orderly moved the gurney forward, toward the entrance. "I'll stay with her after I answer a few questions for the police," Keely told Lucky.

"So will I."

"If you wish, but how is Dr. Rattigan handling all this?" the older woman asked.

"I have no idea."

Reminded that their plans for the future might have been crushed today, Zora felt a twinge of concern. "You should check on him."

"I'll text you when she goes into surgery," Keely volunteered. "They won't let you in, anyway."

Another spasm seized Zora. "Ow!" A curse word slipped out. How did women bear this for hours and hours?

She was very glad she was having a C-section and the doctor would give her something to stop the labor.

As the contraction eased, she wished Lucky would stay. But when he excused himself to attend to his doctor, Zora merely nodded.

"Later," she whispered into the air.

ZORA WAS SAFE. Yes, there were risks in surgery and childbirth, but nothing like what Lucky had feared: a head-on smashup at high speed, pieces of car scattered across the highway, horrifying injuries to the occupants.

He'd witnessed the aftermath of such tragedies as an ambulance driver and a paramedic. The fact that Safe Harbor Medical didn't have an emergency room had added to its appeal when he'd joined the staff, because he didn't have to witness the arrival of trauma patients and relive those terrible memories. But today they'd hit him full force.

I love her, Lucky acknowledged as the gurney vanished into admitting. It was foolish and irrational and inescapable. He had no idea when he'd fallen in love with Zora, or what to do about it.

He'd clung to his ideals of perfection since his parents' deaths. If they had a family at the ideal time and in the ideal circumstances, money problems didn't force parents to neglect their children's internal struggles and teenagers didn't have to work such long hours that they rebelled—or so he'd rationalized.

He'd been trying to control the future, to prevent a repeat of his family's tragedies. But danger could strike without warning, as it had today. How stubbornly blind he'd been to his own flaws, criticizing Zora's illusions while harboring his own.

Yet she was still having another man's babies. Even a slug like Andrew would surely visit them, and there remained a possibility—remote, but real—that she would reconcile with her ex. Lucky might love her so hard and deep that his entire soul throbbed with it, only to have her torn away from him.

He could do nothing about it while she was in surgery. Frustrated, he decided to make himself useful elsewhere.

Since people gathered in a central location in a crisis, Lucky set out for the cafeteria. En route, he passed the elevators, one of which opened to reveal a welcome pair: Karen, her expression worried, and Rod, holding a cold pack to his nose.

Lucky halted. "I hope it's not broken."

"No, fortunately," Karen said. "They X-rayed him and gave him pain pills."

"Hurts to talk," Rod muttered.

Lucky didn't doubt that. "Zora's having the twins. Keely's with her." He filled them in on the details.

"I'm so glad they're okay," Karen said.

"The girls." Rod peered down the hall. "Where are they?"

"Helen said she was going to get them something to eat. Let's try the cafeteria."

Sure enough, they spotted Tiffany and Amber huddled with their grandmother at a table. Doctors, nurses and other staffers were sprinkled around the large room. Although some were eating dinner, most appeared to be waiting for news. Cole looked tense but composed, drinking coffee alongside Dr. Tartikoff.

From the food service area, Jennifer greeted them and asked Rod how he was feeling. Her dark hair was rumpled and her mascara had smeared. Today's events must be a PR director's nightmare.

"Thank you," she said after her questions had been answered. "Now I'm sure you're eager to join your daughters."

Rod agreed, and off he went with Karen. Lucky lingered, unsure where he could help the most.

"Any word about the Adamses?" he asked.

"So far, only that the police are on the scene."

"Well, I have a little more info than that."

She listened intently to the account of Zora and Keely's close call. "Thank heaven they escaped," she said, then raised a hand for silence. "Hang on. I'm monitoring news reports." She listened on her earpiece before saying, "No updates."

"Where's the press?" Lucky had expected to find them crowding the hallways.

"They went haring off to the crash scene," she said. "The police public information officer is handling them, although I'm also receiving calls for our reaction."

"What kind of reaction?" How could anyone respond to such a complex situation?

"Our official position is that our thoughts and prayers are with their family," Jennifer said.

"That sounds right." Lucky admired the publicist more than ever.

"Keep on the alert for stray reporters, will you?" she asked. "We can't let them eavesdrop or hassle people."

"Agreed." While he respected the job of the media, this was a traumatic enough situation without the press breaching people's privacy.

"There should be a counselor on hand. For some reason, I can't reach Laird," Jennifer fretted.

"He's leaving for private practice." Lucky repeated what he'd heard the psychologist announce.

She groaned. "Great timing. I'll arrange for an outside crisis counselor."

A murmur ran through the room. Tony and Mark had just entered. The attorney strode over to the girls' table and spoke in a low voice. The group, including Rod and Karen, got up and accompanied him out.

Lucky's chest clenched. This couldn't be good.

Once the girls and their entourage had departed and

Jennifer gave the all clear from the hall, Mark took a position in full view of everyone. Thanks to his height and deep baritone, he had no trouble commanding attention.

"I'm sure you've heard that Mr. and Mrs. Adams were involved in a single-car crash on Coast Highway," he said. "I've just received word from the police chief that both of them died at the scene."

Gasps and a few sobs rose from the crowd. Even Lucky, angry as he'd been at Vince, was shocked by their deaths. Yet this could have been worse, much worse. Tiff and Amber might have died, too, if he and Rod hadn't prevented the girls' parents from forcing them into the car.

Mark resumed addressing the staff. "For those of you wondering how this will affect the men's fertility program, I'm afraid we don't have an answer on that yet. Any other questions?"

There were a few, which the director fielded with complete frankness. Then a buzz of conversation broke out as staffers shared their grief with each other.

At a tap on his arm, Lucky swung around to meet Betsy Raditch's solemn gaze. "I heard Zora's having her babies," she said. "Have you talked to her?"

"Yes. Did you know she and Keely had a near miss on the road?"

"What do you mean?"

He repeated the story. The nursing supervisor clamped her hand over her mouth. "That was close!"

"She should be in surgery now," Lucky added.

"I'll tell Andrew," Betsy said. "And, Lucky, I heard what you did, keeping Rod's daughters safe. That was heroic."

"Thanks, but I don't deserve that," Lucky responded. "Heroes are people who risk their safety, like Rod. I knew I was a match for that—" in view of Vince's demise, he decided against using a harsh term "—that man."

"You and Rod both deserve credit," the nursing supervisor said. "Well, I'd better get moving. Some of my nurses are in shock, and we have a hospital to run."

"Absolutely right." If Lucky had a supervisory position like hers, he'd be eager to support his nurses, too.

Outside the cafeteria, Cole caught up with him. "We're holding a strategy session in Dr. Tartikoff's office. You should be part of it."

"I'd like that." Lucky joined his doctor and a handful of others. To be included with this prestigious group was an honor, and his future might depend on what they devised.

All the same, en route to the fifth floor, his thoughts were mostly on Zora. She'd been his collaborator this past month, as invested as he was in trying to ensure the billionaire's gift. All she'd requested was for him to stop nagging her.

She'd kept Vince's hateful harassment a secret, no doubt to prevent this type of blowup. What had she gained by it? Her position and her advancement didn't depend on the program's expansion.

She did it for me. From simple generosity, or because she hadn't been able to bear the prospect of Lucky leaving? Had Zora started loving him, too, perhaps without realizing it?

If Andrew reached her first, would she still fail to recognize that her heart belonged to Lucky?

Suddenly he couldn't wait to be with her. But Dr. Rattigan was counting on Lucky's input.

He steeled himself to have patience. In view of Andrew's track record, there was no reason to assume he'd show up promptly.

The distinguished group of top staffers, including several whom Owen Tartikoff had brought with him from his Boston practice, gathered around the conference table in the fertility director's office. They included Alec Denny, the director of laboratories, and Jan Garcia Sargent, head of the egg donor program.

For the next hour, they brainstormed, tossing out the names of distinguished foundations, government grant programs and Silicon Valley billionaires. Could or would any of them respond—let alone quickly enough to purchase the dental building?

Just as they were about to call it a night, the administrator entered. Dr. Rayburn's dark eyes were rimmed with red.

"Have a seat." Lucky vacated his chair, since all the others were taken.

The big man accepted the offer. "Considering you're a hero, I shouldn't, but I've had a rough day. As we all have."

Lucky decided not to bother arguing about the hero designation. No one questioned it, so apparently they'd all heard the tale.

"On such a terrible day, I'm pleased to bring good news." When Mark coughed, Lucky fetched him a glass of water from the sideboard. The administrator swallowed a few gulps before continuing. "Portia's mother, Helen Pepper, is a very kind woman. In the midst of her grief, she informed me that her daughter and son-in-law placed their estate in a living trust. They designated her as the successor trustee on behalf of the couple's children."

Lucky had assumed Vince's money would be tied up for a year or more as the estate was settled. Without a living trust, probate in California could be a lengthy, expensive and complicated process.

"She and her granddaughters intend to carry out the Adamses' wishes to donate twenty million dollars to our program." A smile broke through Mark's weariness. "And a million dollars to the Oahu Lane Animal Shelter, which appears to be a favorite of the girls."

Around the table, the others expressed relief and gratitude. "I hate to raise the question, but how soon can this happen?" Cole asked. "That building will be snapped up quickly."

"Helen plans to talk to an attorney tomorrow." Mark downed more water. "She's agreed to let Jennifer Martin and Ms. Yashimoto arrange the funeral while she looks into setting up a foundation to underwrite the men's program. She said that having her daughter and son-in-law's names on the building will be a fitting tribute."

Lucky was pleased that they'd include Portia's name. She deserved it.

The news buoyed the exhausted participants, though no one was happy about the circumstances. The impact of today's events would play out in everyone's emotions for a long time, including Lucky's.

A glance at his watch sent his heart speeding off. Several hours had passed since he'd last seen Zora. He'd received texts from Keely, indicating the C-section had gone well. By now, the new mom should be out of the recovery room, which meant he'd finally be able to visit.

After excusing himself, he hurried down to the third floor. Despite his eagerness to reach Zora, the window of the intermediate care nursery drew him irresistibly.

He spotted Melissa and Edmond's triplets—had it really been only two nights since their birth?—and a sprinkling of other newborns. Among the half dozen babies in clear isolettes, he wasn't sure which were Zora's, but if he had to bet, he'd put his money on a red-haired little girl and the blond boy beside her. Both appeared alert and healthy.

At the nurses' station, Lucky obtained Zora's room number. "Mr. Raditch is with her," a nurse advised him.

A lump stuck in Lucky's throat. He hadn't thought Andrew would arrive so fast.

Why was he here? To stake his claim? He *was* the babies' father. But it was his claim on *Zora* that worried Lucky most.

It was up to her whether she would reconcile with Andrew, but Lucky didn't intend to let her go without a fight. He'd waited too long already to realize that she was the perfect woman for him.

Chapter Eighteen

The first thing that occurred to Zora when her ex-husband entered was, *You're the wrong man.*

She longed for Lucky's honest, caring presence. Why hadn't she told him she wanted him to stay with her, that he was the most important person in her life? Sure, it meant taking a big emotional risk. Maybe he'd never accept her, flaws and all, but something about the way he gazed at her said otherwise. She'd taken leaps of faith, over and over, with the unworthy Andrew. Now she'd let Lucky go off without asking for what meant the most to her—keeping him close.

He must be busy, though, with the hospital in an uproar. Keely had brought news of Vince and Portia's deaths, and the two women had shared their turbulent reactions. Zora supposed the aftermath would affect her for a long while. Her heart went out to Tiffany and Amber on the loss of their mother, but mostly she was thankful she and Keely had escaped injury.

After Keely left for dinner, Edmond had peeked in. He'd been visiting his wife and triplets, and stayed just long enough to express his best wishes and present a gorgeous bouquet that perfumed the room.

And now here was her ex-husband. "So you had the babies." Andrew hovered near the exit as if fearing a giant clamp might drop from the ceiling to hold him in place, forcing him to—what?—take responsibility? "They look, uh, cute."

That was the sum of his reaction? When Zora had cradled the babies after their delivery, their delicate scent and wonder-filled faces had instantly become engraved on her heart. Elizabeth had a tumble of reddish-brown hair and inquisitive gray eyes, while the boy was blond with bright blue eyes. As she crooned to each of them, she'd been rewarded with a gaze of pure devotion.

She'd have died for them. Their father thought they were, *uh, cute*.

Andrew shifted from one foot to the other. "Have you picked names?"

"The girl's Elizabeth."

"Like my mother."

"That's right." She waited, wondering if he had ideas about the boy's name. What a silly fantasy she'd harbored, that he would leap at the chance, yet the moment had played through her mind so often that it almost seemed real: Andrew declaring that he'd always loved the name something-or-other, or that he couldn't wait to take Elizabeth and what's-his-name to the zoo. When he didn't speak, she blurted, "I might call the boy Luke." That ought to get his attention.

"Okay." Obviously, Andrew hadn't connected the name to Lucky. Maybe he was too busy preparing his next revelation, which was: "I'm transferring to New York."

He was moving out of state? That seemed sudden. "When?"

"Next month."

"Permanently?"

"That's the idea."

Once, this news would have arrowed pain deep into Zora's gut. Now, she experienced relief tinged with sadness for this self-absorbed man. He would never do anything more important than fathering these children, yet clearly he didn't intend to play much of a role in their upbringing. As she'd suspected, his bid for custody had been merely an attempt to one-up her.

"Good luck with that." She didn't bother to point out that states enforced each other's child-support requirements. Her lawyer could take care of the details.

"Do me a favor, would you?" Andrew muttered.

Warily, she asked, "What?"

"Let my mom play with the kids once in a while. She's into this grandmother thing."

He'd been around Zora since they were teenagers, yet he believed she might exclude Betsy? "You don't know me at all," she said.

"Is that a yes?" He sounded like a sales agent impatient to conclude a deal.

Zora lifted her head from the pillow for a better view of the man who used to dominate her world. Yep, he'd definitely shrunk. "Okay," she said. "Thanks for stopping by."

Andrew regarded her with a shade of disappointment. "That's it?"

He must have expected her to plead for him to stay in Safe Harbor. After Lin's rejection, his ego was hungry to be fed. "That's it. Sayonara."

He glared at her. "Whatever," he said, and stalked out.

The air smelled suddenly fresher, and the colors of the flowers intensified. Then the best thing of all happened.

Lucky peered in. Although his face could use a splash of water and his navy blue uniform had picked up bits of lint, he was the handsomest man in the world.

THE DISMAY ON Andrew's face as he stomped down the hall thrilled Lucky. "You knocked him down to size," he told Zora admiringly as he entered her room. "You're such a tiny thing but wow, you pack a punch."

She lifted an eyebrow. "You're just figuring that out?"

Careful to avoid jostling her, Lucky sat on the edge of the bed. "Among other things. A lot of them."

Including that his image of a perfect wife and kids had been nothing more than a defense mechanism to protect against the kind of devastation that had torn his family apart. That his delusion about controlling the future was as self-defeating as anything he'd accused her of. That he didn't see how he could go through life without this delightful, maddening woman.

"Did you figure out yet that you're in love with me?" As soon as the words flew out, blood rushed to her cheeks. "Oops. I didn't mean to say that aloud."

Lucky nearly bounced off the bed in glee. "Yes, I'm in love with you. Now tell me you're in love with me, too."

"Um…I have to think about it."

"Zora!" He could barely tolerate the delay.

She folded her arms. "What other things did you figure out today, smart guy?"

"That you have the most precious children in the world." Lucky visualized the babies again. "Your twins are the red-headed girl and the blond boy, right? I couldn't read the names on the isolettes."

Her face remained adorably flushed, this time with pride rather than embarrassment, he guessed. "Elizabeth and Luke."

Lucky couldn't have heard correctly. "You're giving him my name?"

"I'm trying it on for size." Zora shifted against the pillow.

Much as Lucky cherished the idea, it wouldn't be fair to the boy. "He should have his own name," he said. "How about Orlando?"

"Like the city in Florida?"

"Like my father." He'd meant to reserve that honor for his firstborn son. Well, this little guy had taken over that spot in Lucky's heart.

"I might go for that," Zora responded. "But if you name him, you might have to claim him."

"I'm claiming both of them." Lucky smiled at the dear, freckled person studying him expectantly.

"You don't still consider them Andrew's children?"

Her question startled him. "I consider them *your* children. I meant that *you* considered them Andrew's children."

"Really?"

"I believed you might forgive him for past sins if he, shall we say, embraced the miracle of fatherhood."

Zora's nose wrinkled. "I was an idiot. I believed love could conquer all, but it can't conquer heartlessness. Or a weak character. Or—should I go on abusing him, or is that enough?"

"For now, because I have something important to say." Lucky gathered his courage. "Let's get back to the part where I confess I'm in love with you."

Why didn't she respond in kind? But perhaps she was waiting for him to lay out the whole picture. Well, he'd better start by being cautious. Although it appeared Lucky might be able to stay in Safe Harbor, there was no guarantee he'd be hired in the new program. He might not be as hung up on financial security as before, but he couldn't ask for a commitment from Zora without pointing out that his situation was still unsettled.

"Another thing I discovered today was that I couldn't bear to leave Safe Harbor unless you go with me," he blurted. "Will you?"

"You have to go?" Her joy dimmed. "But…that means leaving our friends."

"I'll make it worth your while."

"I'd go with you in a heartbeat," Zora answered. "Except…"

"What?" His breath caught.

"My sister did that and ended up unmarried and un-loved." She stared down at her hands.

"Such trust," he murmured.

She folded her arms and hunkered down.

His impatience nearly exploded. But what did he expect, reassurance before he popped the question? *Put it out there, fella. Quit stalling.*

From the zipper compartment in his wallet, Lucky produced a gold ring set with diamonds and emeralds. Then he slid off the bed and onto one knee. "Zora, will you marry me?"

She stared at him in astonishment. "What about your perfect family?"

He pushed past the lump in his throat. "You are my perfect family. You, Elizabeth and Orlando."

"But your plans…saving for a house…"

"I nearly lost you today," he said. "That put everything into perspective. I want you today, and tomorrow, and forever. Marry me, Zora."

"Yes."

"Yes?" He couldn't quite believe she'd said it so simply and plainly. "No ifs, ands or buts?"

"Don't be silly. I love you."

"I love you, too!" Hoisting himself onto the bed again, he showered kisses on her forehead and cheeks and mouth.

Chuckling, she held up the ring. "Let me put this on."

He straightened. "Of course."

As she angled it toward her finger, her forehead creased. "Where did you… This looks familiar."

"I borrowed it from Betsy." Lucky had run into the nursing supervisor in the hall and shared his plans. When he mentioned that he wished he had a token ring to present until he had a chance to buy a new one, Betsy had removed the heirloom from her finger and loaned it to him.

"Did she mention that I wore this ring during my marriage to Andrew?" Zora asked, laughing.

"She left out that part." Lucky sighed, sorry that he'd screwed up such an important detail. "I was planning for us to choose our rings together later."

Zora studied it fondly. "It's beautiful and it means a lot to Betsy. How sweet of her to loan it to us."

"This doesn't change your answer, does it? We *are* engaged, right?"

"You bet."

Sliding his arms around Zora, he leaned down for a long, tender kiss. She smelled of babies and happiness. Lucky's heart swelled as her arms closed around him and the two of them hung there, happily suspended in a private world.

A world they would share with their little guys. A world that would be full of bumps and twists and imperfections, exactly as it ought to be.

"For the record, I came to the conclusion that we loved each other long before you did," she whispered in his ear. "It didn't occur to you until today? Slow, slow."

Lucky grinned. "Guess I am. By the way, there's an excellent chance we won't have to leave Safe Harbor." Releasing her, he explained about Helen's proposal to fund the expansion.

"That's fantastic." Zora tapped her fingers together restlessly.

"What?" he asked.

"Maybe I shouldn't bring this up now."

"Let it out," Lucky told her. "If you have reservations, now's your chance to air them."

"It's not exactly a reservation."

"What is it?" He stroked her hair. Whatever the problem was, they'd deal with it.

"Your brother," Zora said.

Lucky blinked. He hadn't been expecting *that*. "What about him?"

"Do you still reject him for whatever he did?" she said earnestly. "Are you still so rigid?"

Despite an urge to protest that he could never forgive what Matthew had done, Lucky paused to reflect. This past month, he'd learned a lot from Zora's generous nature. While her weakness for Andrew had infuriated him, she'd also befriended Lin Lee, mended fences with Zady and regained her closeness with Betsy. He could use some of her grace.

"I'd like to tell you what happened," he said.

Zora gripped his hands. "Please do."

As Lucky began, the hospital faded around him and he was once more in his parents' convenience store in LA. He could hear the street traffic and smell the salty temptation of potato chips. When he looked up, a security mirror revealed a bulging image of shelves crammed with the odds and ends of a neighborhood market.

"My brother Matthew joined the navy at eighteen," he said. "I was proud of him, but that left me to juggle attending high school and helping my folks keep the store afloat." He'd unloaded supplies, stocked shelves, carried receipts to the bank and fetched change. He'd also operated the cash register many evenings late into the night.

"It must have been hard, missing school activities," Zora said.

"Yes, and I longed for the occasional evening to hang out with my friends." Lucky felt a twinge of his old resentment. "I rebelled in small ways. Sneaking a cigarette, showing up late or leaving early. Mom used to scowl and Dad complained that I was letting down the family while my brother risked his life for his country."

"How did you feel about that?" she asked.

"Guilty, but angry, too." In retrospect, his selfishness haunted him. Still, he owed her the whole truth. "One evening, we were supposed to close at nine, but my mother insisted on staying open late because customers kept drifting in. While she worked the register, she sent me into the storage room to open boxes of supplies we'd received that day and catalog the contents. I was furious."

"Where was your father?"

"He'd put in twelve hours and gone home exhausted." Lucky's gut twisted. "If I smoked on the premises, my mom would smell it. So I sneaked out the rear door into the alley."

Strange—he'd relived that night repeatedly in nightmares, yet now he had trouble dredging up the details. *Get it over with.*

"While I was outside, a junkie entered the store and demanded cash from my mother," he said. "The store surveillance tape showed he had a bulge in his jacket, but not whether it was a gun."

"How terrifying." Zora's gaze never strayed from Lucky's face. "What happened?"

"My mom collapsed." Lucky swallowed. "Later, the coroner said she died from stress cardiomyopathy, which is a response to overwhelming fear. A huge jolt of adrenaline can cause the heart to develop ventricular fibrillation—abnormal rhythms. She literally dropped dead."

Zora shivered. "I'm sorry. But you weren't at fault."

"If I'd been inside, I might have heard the robbery, rushed in and scared the creep away," Lucky said. "Maybe before Mom succumbed."

"If he did have a gun, he'd have killed you," she countered.

"I doubt he did." Lucky refused to let himself off that easily. "Anyway, he snatched a handful of cash and ran."

"Did they catch him?"

"More or less." His jaw tightened. "He was a meth addict—a couple of days later the police found him dead of an overdose, probably with drugs he bought at my mother's expense."

"And that didn't bring her back," she observed sympathetically.

"No, it didn't." The discovery of his mother lying on the floor, the sirens, the arrival of police and paramedics had blurred into a montage of pain. Worst of all had been accompanying the police to inform his sleepy, disbelieving father.

Lucky had feared his father might collapse, too. Instead, Orlando Mendez had thrown himself into his work. "He gave his all to that store. I offered to postpone college and put in longer hours, but he refused. Instead, he hired an assistant. Nearly a year later, we discovered the assistant was embezzling from us."

"That's terrible." Zora stroked his arm.

Lucky had had trouble believing anyone could take advantage of people who were already suffering. Sadly, he and his father had learned otherwise.

"The guy fled to South America and we never recovered the money. A month after that, Dad died of an aneurysm," Lucky said grimly. "Literally, of a broken heart. I had to sell the store. There was barely enough to cover the debts and the funeral expenses."

That brought him to the bitter quarrel with Matthew. When his brother had attended their mother's funeral, he'd scarcely spoken. After their father's death, Matthew had blown up at Lucky.

"He accused me of contributing to our parents' deaths." Although the years had lessened his outrage, the memory stung. "He claimed I cheated him of his inheritance, that I'd used the profits from the sale of the store to pay for college. He even filed a theft report with the police. After they cleared me, Matthew informed our relatives I'd hidden the money and gotten away with it."

"Wow," Zora said. "That puts my quarrel with Zady in the shade."

As she spoke, guilt and regret flooded through Lucky.

"If I hadn't been such an immature jerk, we might have avoided the argument. In a way, he was right. I let everyone down with my irresponsible actions the night my mother died. And I vowed that I'd never do that again to anyone I cared about, yet I let you down with Vince."

"What?" Astonishment filled Zora's face.

To his dismay, a sob shook Lucky. He never cried. He was the strong one, the tough guy. But the idea that Zora had put up with that man's groping in order to protect Lucky's career was intolerable. "I'm glad he's dead. I'm sorry about his wife, but…" His hands formed fists. "I messed up. And I had the nerve to rag on you about *your* mistakes."

"Yeah, that was the worst thing. I mean, death and destruction and being estranged from your brother hardly count compared to your nagging."

Her mischievous tone had the desired effect of banishing his self-pity. "You little goof."

Zora reached out to cup his cheek. "You're a wonderful man, Lucky. You've carried this burden for too long. I don't think you need to forgive your brother as much as you need to forgive yourself."

"I let everyone down. I can't undo that." Her touch soothed him, though.

"How many people did you save as a paramedic?" she asked. "And according to what I heard, if not for you, Rod's daughters might have died today. You were a kid when you sneaked out for a smoke. I don't know if you can mend the rift with Matthew, but as for the rest, let it go, Lucky."

Relief spread through him, a healing balm. "When did you get so smart?"

"When I fell in love with the right man," she said.

Lucky hugged her again, careful of her surgical wound. "You don't mind sharing a house with Karen and Rod? We could rent an apartment."

"I'd rather stay there, if it's okay with you," she said. "It's like having a big family."

"I agree." While it might not be possible for that family to include his brother, Lucky intended to try.

They were starting fresh, a man and woman who'd stumbled and screwed up plenty. Yet the future gleamed ahead of them in rainbow colors, because together they were stronger and wiser than separately.

They'd have a lot more fun, too.

Chapter Nineteen

The adobe house had neatly trimmed bushes and a red tile roof, with striped woven curtains tied back at the windows. Mounting the porch steps, Lucky rubbed his damp palms on his jeans.

In response to his inquiry, a cousin had emailed that Matthew was stationed here in Point Hueneme, a few hours' drive to the north of Safe Harbor. Lucky hadn't even been sure how to say the town's name, which he'd learned on the internet was pronounced WY-nee-mee.

When he'd phoned, Matthew had cautiously agreed to meet with him. He'd suggested meeting at his house today while his wife and school-age children were attending a birthday party.

It might have been more sensible to choose a public place, Lucky mused. What if his brother threw a punch at him?

Well, he hadn't slammed down the phone or insulted Lucky. Although his tone had been wary, Lucky's mood was cautious, too.

Not finding a bell, he knocked, then wiped his palms on his pants again. Had Zora been this nervous when she'd prepared herself to see her sister? She must have waited like this, uncertain, anxious...

The door opened. Sixteen years had matured Matthew's olive face. He was, surprisingly, a couple of inches shorter

than Lucky— *I must have grown.* Yet in every other respect, despite the passage of time, Matthew was incredibly
familiar. In a rush, Lucky realized how much he'd missed
the pal who'd taught him to play baseball when their dad
was too busy and had advised him on which classes to
choose in high school.

"Thanks for agreeing to meet me," Lucky said.

Matthew extended a strong, callused hand. They shook,
and then his brother pulled him close and clapped his
shoulder. "I'm glad you had the guts to make the first
move."

"Damn," Lucky said. "If I start to cry, I'll be embarrassed."

"Nothing to be ashamed of." Releasing him, his brother
moved aside to let him enter.

A couch and comfortable chairs, along with a book-
shelf, TV and game system, filled the living room. On
the wall hung a red, black and buff ceramic Aztec calendar almost identical to Lucky's. "Hey, we have the same
interior decorator."

Matthew followed his gaze to the plaque. "It's like the
one Grandpa and Grandma used to have."

"I'd forgotten."

"Aunt Maria and Uncle Carlos own it now. Man, I'm
sorry." Matthew stood squarely balanced on both feet, his
khaki T-shirt emphasizing the breadth of his chest and
shoulders. "You should have been at those family gatherings all these years."

Their grandparents had died before their parents, so
Lucky hadn't been denied the chance to say goodbye to
them at least. As for the aunts and uncles, it had been their
decision to exclude him without hearing his side. "I'm fine.
Just got engaged, in fact."

"Fantastic!" Matt raised his hands to signal he had more
to say. "Let me get this out. I nursed my anger at you for
years, until gradually it dawned on me that I was angry

about a lot of things that had nothing to do with you. At myself for not being there when our parents needed me. Also at leaving you to carry the burden. I worked such long hours that I ran off to join the navy to get away from the store."

Lucky had never suspected that his brother's motives in enlisting had included escape. Not that he blamed Matthew. "I resented working so hard, too. That's why I sneaked out for cigarettes, which was totally irresponsible. I should have been there with Mom that night."

"I wasn't there, either. Even though I'm proud to serve my country, I signed up partly for the wrong reasons." His brother shook his head. "The other day, looking at some new recruits, I noticed how young they were, and it hit me you were about that age when our parents died."

"Eighteen," Lucky recalled. "Grown-up."

Matt tilted his head. "A baby."

"So were you when you enlisted."

"That's no excuse for my behavior." A crooked smile brightened his brother's face. "Enough beating ourselves up. Can we put this in the past?"

"That's why I'm here," Lucky said.

"Tell me about this fiancée of yours," his brother said.

"I'll show you a picture." He took out his phone.

Soon they were lounging on the furniture, downing soft drinks and catching up on everything they'd missed.

"YOU'VE NEVER BEEN able to fix a pie crust as beautiful as mine." Playfully, Zady indicated the luscious apple pie on a side table reserved for Thanksgiving desserts. "I admit, your pecan pie looks yummy, but your crust isn't as shiny. The secret is to brush the unbaked crust with an egg mixed with a couple of tablespoons of cream."

Zora gave her sister a poke. They'd turned their old rivalry into friendly teasing since Zady had moved to town a few weeks earlier. "Insult it all you like. Lucky bought the pecan pie at the supermarket."

"You're kidding! You didn't bake your own pie?" Zady chuckled. "Mom would have a cow."

"Feel free to tell her."

"I doubt she's speaking to either of us since we informed her of your wedding after the fact."

At the reminder, Zora gazed happily down at the ring Lucky had placed there a week earlier. Although he'd offered to buy a more expensive one, she preferred this simple, classic design in gold. "I'm not sure which bothered her most, that I didn't invite her or that you served as my maid of honor."

She'd been a little saddened not to be able to include her mother. But after Mom's drunken behavior at Zora's first wedding and her cruel manipulations with Zady, Zora had stuck to her resolve to keep some distance between them. Afterward, she'd written her mother informing her of her marriage and asking for her blessing. There'd been no reply.

The wedding at the county's picturesque Old Courthouse had been modest but magical, thanks to the love flowing between the bride and groom. And they'd been surrounded by friends and family. While Betsy and Keely held the twins, Zady had served as maid of honor and Matthew as best man. Zora had immediately liked Matthew, as well as his dark-haired wife and children. They planned to hold another reunion at Christmas.

"Are you ladies squabbling?" Lucky's arm around Zora's waist restored her to the present. "You'll set a bad example for our children."

"It'll teach them to stick up for themselves," she countered, and rested her cheek on his shoulder. "Besides, Zady and I don't fight any more. Just a little sisterly competition."

"That's okay, then."

What a wonderful man she'd married, she thought, nestling against Lucky.

As for a honeymoon, that was on hold until the babies were old enough to wean and leave with others. When she and her husband took a trip, there'd be no interruptions, however cute.

"These little guys are ready for their nap." From the den, Betsy brought Orlando into the kitchen, yawning in his hand-crocheted blanket. On her finger glittered the ring that would always remind Zora of their close connection.

"Elizabeth's dozing, too." Keely cradled her precious charge.

"Much as I adore them, thank goodness they're asleep." Breast-feeding two babies consumed more energy than Zora had imagined, and she was grateful for the help. "I'm starving."

The aroma of roast turkey and stuffing had been wafting from the kitchen all afternoon. Tiffany and Amber had insisted on pitching in to help Karen cook, while Rod and Grandma Helen arranged the dining room.

"Upstairs we go," Betsy said. "Keely?"

The nurse gave a start. "Of course." Head lowered, she hurried after the older woman.

Keely had been acting distracted since the wedding. Guiltily, Zora reflected that she hadn't been paying much attention to her friend.

For a while, Keely had been upbeat, buoyed by the news of Laird's departure. As his replacement, the hospital had hired a family and child counselor named Franca Brightman, whom Edmond had recommended. Already, she was helping the Adams girls adjust to their loss.

But since the wedding, Keely had retreated into long silences. Now that Zora was on leave and no longer required rides to work, they had less chance to speak privately.

Today was hardly the occasion for a tête-à-tête, but Zora resolved to find a moment alone with Keely later. Perhaps she was suffering a posttraumatic reaction to their brush with death, or struggling to adjust to the many changes at the hospital.

With the purchase of the dental building, buzz filled the halls about the planned renovations and new staff to be hired. Exciting though it was, Zora remembered all the disruptions over the past few years as the hospital had been transformed. Perhaps that had contributed to Keely's downcast mood.

Her stomach growled as Tiffany and Amber paraded in and set hot dishes on the breakfast table, which would be used for serving. "I wish we lived here instead of at Grandma's," Amber said as she placed a casserole carefully on the tablecloth.

Tiffany glanced around. No sign of Helen. "I love Grandma, but honestly, we're underfoot in her house." Helen owned a two-bedroom cottage a few miles away.

"Especially with her arthritis," the younger girl added. "She's always cleaning up after us. I try to be neat but hey, I'm a kid."

Although newfound wealth had enabled Helen to hire a housekeeper to shop, cook and handle major cleaning, hosting a pair of active granddaughters was taking its toll, Zora had noted from the older woman's increasingly stiff movements. However, she respected that Helen chose not to buy a mansion or invest in more staff. She insisted on keeping the girls in touch with reality. In addition to sharing a bedroom, they would be transferring to public school next year.

Also, Tiff had enrolled in a dance class. Amber, who had loved to swim competitively until Vince turned every meet into a do-or-die situation, was easing into the sport again.

Partly to assist Helen, Rod had offered to relinquish his room to them and move in with Karen. The grandmother had replied firmly that she couldn't let the girls grow up in a home with a pair of unmarried adults sharing a bed.

Karen brought out a bowl of mashed potatoes, and Rod followed with a platter of sliced turkey. His daughters hurried into the kitchen to collect the salad and stuffing.

Helen joined them, along with Betsy and Keely. That was the whole group for today—Melissa, Edmond, Dawn and the triplets were dining with his parents, while Jack, Anya and their baby had flown to Colorado to share the holiday with her large family.

"I put the monitor by my place in the dining room," Keely told Zora. "That way, if the babies fuss, I can check on them. If you don't mind."

"Mind?" Zora repeated. "You're doing me a favor!"

"No problem." Keely avoided her eyes.

Before Zora could question her friend, she felt Lucky's hand on her spine, propelling her toward the food. "Serve yourself first. You're a nursing mommy."

Amid a chorus of agreement, she complied. Soon they were all seated, and after a prayer of gratitude for this special gathering, they dug into their heaped-high plates.

What a year it had been, Zora thought as she took in the beloved faces around the table. When a group of friends had moved into this house last February, they'd had no idea that by the end of November, there would be six babies born and three marriages.

"Have you found an apartment yet, Zady?" Betsy asked amid the chatter. Zora's sister was staying in a small unit at the Harbor Suites.

"Nothing I really love," Zady admitted.

Keely toyed with her food. In contrast to the others, she appeared to have little appetite for her meal.

Zora shot her a concerned glance. Keely ignored it.

"Can we have dessert?" Amber indicated the plate she'd cleaned at top speed.

"Where are your manners?" reproved her grandmother. "Not till everyone's finished."

"How about the pumpkin bread?" Amber persisted. "That isn't really dessert, is it, Grandma?"

"I suppose not." Seated between her granddaughters, Helen acquiesced fondly. "Why don't you bring in the plate for everyone?"

"I'll get it." To Zora's surprise, Rod sprang up. Usually the anesthesiologist moved at a slower pace than everyone else, and he'd milked his injured nose for sympathy until the bruising faded. He whisked out of the room, and Zora heard a cabinet open and shut in the kitchen.

"What's Dad doing?" Amber asked.

"I guess we'll find out," Tiffany said.

The slightly built man returned, jauntily hoisting the plate of pumpkin bread. When he set it in front of Karen, Zora saw a miniature van displayed in the center.

"What's this?" Their landlady lifted the little vehicle to inspect it.

"It's the first part of my surprise." Rod stood next to her, bouncing with anticipation. "That's a stand-in for the van I'm buying. I'll be taking delivery of it next week. It carries eight, so we can drive the girls and their friends. Helen, I made sure it was accessible for you to get in and out of."

"That's lovely." She sounded puzzled, though, and Zora suspected they all were. Why display this in the middle of Thanksgiving dinner?

"The doors and hood open," Rod prompted.

"It would be hard to drive it otherwise." Beside Zora, Lucky smirked at the other man.

Instead of riposting as he usually would, Rod cleared his throat. "I mean the miniature. Open the hood."

With a bemused expression, their landlady tipped it open and gasped. "Oh, Rod!"

"What is it? What is it?" The girls crowded around.

Karen held up a diamond engagement ring. "My gosh."

Rod dipped, suggestive of lowering himself to one knee, although he never quite touched the floor. "Will you make an honest man of me?"

Karen's mouth hung open. Then she gathered her wits. "Of course I will, you crazy man!" To the girls' cheers, she kissed him.

Zora could have sworn Helen's smile revealed a hint of relief. This meant the girls could move in with their father and new stepmother, while living only a few miles from their grandma.

"Congratulations." Betsy seemed as thrilled as the rest of them.

A soft sob on Zora's far side riveted her gaze to Keely. The woman appeared to be fighting tears.

"What's wrong?" Surely the nurse hadn't fallen in love with Rod. Zora had seen no sign of it.

"I don't mean to spoil the happy occasion." She sucked in air.

"Calm down and share what's bothering you," Zora urged. "Please."

Glumly, Keely answered. "You're all families now. Of course your sister should live here, too."

"Why?" Zady asked.

Keely didn't have to answer, because Zora understood. "You've been expecting us to ask you to leave?"

The older nurse nodded.

"No way," Lucky said.

"You belong here," Karen chimed in.

"She's your twin," Keely said doggedly. "It's only right."

Zora wished she'd addressed this issue long ago. It simply hadn't occurred to her. "You saved my life. The twins' lives, too."

Zady spoke up, too. "Keely, my sister and I have been feuding for years. Yeah, we love each other and we're friends again, but share a house? We'd be at each other's throats in five seconds."

"Blood on the floor," Lucky said calmly.

"No, you wouldn't." Keely refused to be comforted. "You're a member of her family, and I'm not."

"I can fix that," Zora said. "I hereby dub you the babies' honorary aunt. You are therefore a relative. And we love you."

There was a chorus of agreement. "Including me," Rod put in. "Don't tell anybody at work."

Keely joined in the ripple of laughter that greeted this remark. "Really?"

"Really," Zora said.

"Will you help me plan my wedding?" Karen asked. "Since my mother died last year, I've been wishing I had more family."

"You have?" Keely sniffled.

Their landlady gazed dreamily around the table. "Growing up, I wished I had a houseful of brothers and sisters, and other relatives to celebrate holidays. My wish has come true. Keely, you have a home here as long as you want it."

The nurse appeared too choked up to speak.

"Can we eat dessert now?" Amber asked.

"That's the best idea I've heard all day," Lucky said. "Aside from Rod and Karen getting married, and Keely becoming an honorary aunt to our children."

Zora couldn't have agreed more.

* * * * *

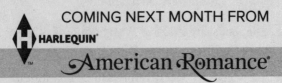

REQUEST YOUR FREE BOOKS!
2 FREE NOVELS PLUS 2 FREE GIFTS!

HARLEQUIN®

American ★ Romance®

LOVE, HOME & HAPPINESS

YES! Please send me 2 FREE Harlequin® American Romance® novels and my 2 FREE gifts (gifts are worth about $10). After receiving them, if I don't wish to receive any more books, I can return the shipping statement marked "cancel." If I don't cancel, I will receive 4 brand-new novels every month and be billed just $4.74 per book in the U.S. or $5.24 per book in Canada. That's a savings of at least 14% off the cover price! It's quite a bargain! Shipping and handling is just 50¢ per book in the U.S. and 75¢ per book in Canada.* I understand that accepting the 2 free books and gifts places me under no obligation to buy anything. I can always return a shipment and cancel at any time. Even if I never buy another book, the two free books and gifts are mine to keep forever.

154/354 HDN F4YN

Name	(PLEASE PRINT)

Address	Apt. #

City	State/Prov.	Zip/Postal Code

Signature (if under 18, a parent or guardian must sign)

Mail to the Harlequin® Reader Service:
IN U.S.A.: P.O. Box 1867, Buffalo, NY 14240-1867
IN CANADA: P.O. Box 609, Fort Erie, Ontario L2A 5X3

Want to try two free books from another line?
Call 1-800-873-8635 or visit www.ReaderService.com.

* Terms and prices subject to change without notice. Prices do not include applicable taxes. Sales tax applicable in N.Y. Canadian residents will be charged applicable taxes. Offer not valid in Quebec. This offer is limited to one order per household. Not valid for current subscribers to Harlequin American Romance books. All orders subject to credit approval. Credit or debit balances in a customer's account(s) may be offset by any other outstanding balance owed by or to the customer. Please allow 4 to 6 weeks for delivery. Offer available while quantities last.

Your Privacy—The Harlequin® Reader Service is committed to protecting your privacy. Our Privacy Policy is available online at www.ReaderService.com or upon request from the Harlequin Reader Service.

We make a portion of our mailing list available to reputable third parties that offer products we believe may interest you. If you prefer that we not exchange your name with third parties, or if you wish to clarify or modify your communication preferences, please visit us at www.ReaderService.com/consumerschoice or write to us at Harlequin Reader Service Preference Service, P.O. Box 9062, Buffalo, NY 14269. Include your complete name and address.

HARI3R

Egan Rebel is the last man Rachel Hollister expects to meet when she returns home to Horseshoe, Texas!

Read on for a sneak peek of
TEXAS REBELS: EGAN, the first book in
Linda Warren's
TEXAS REBELS miniseries.

Rachel Hollister was lost.

For over an hour she'd been traveling this country back road and the scenery had changed from mesquite and scrub to thick woods. She'd left the blacktop some time ago and now the road narrowed to merely a track. She looked around for signs of human life, a barn, anything. But all she saw were woods and more woods where the track ended.

She reached for her phone in her purse and tried to call her brother. No signal. She looked out the window and couldn't see power lines. Where was she? Rachel got out of the car and an eerie feeling came over her. She tried her phone again. Nothing. A sliver of alarm shot through her. How was she going to get out of here? She'd have to walk out or sit here and wait for someone to find her. From the silence, she feared that wait might be long. Her choices were simple. She looked down at her dress and heels. Not ideal for walking. Her suitcase was in the backseat, so she'd just change into jeans and sneakers, she decided.

As Rachel moved toward the door, something caught her eye. Her heart thumped against her chest. There was a man emerging from the woods. He was hard to see because he seemed as one with his surroundings. A duster like she'd seen cowboys wear in olden days flapped around his legs. His dark hair brushed against his collar, and he had at least a day's worth of stubble. A worn hat was pulled low over his eyes, but what held her attention was the rifle in his hand.

Fear crept along her nerves as she got back into the car, locking the doors manually. The man continued to stride toward her. There was nothing she could do but wait. Who was he? And what was he doing out here so far from anywhere?

Her eyes were glued to him as he drew closer. She scooted away from the window, as if that would help, but when he tapped on the window she jumped, she was so nervous.

"Are you okay, ma'am?"

Don't miss TEXAS REBELS: EGAN *by Linda Warren,*
available April 2015 wherever
Harlequin® American Romance®
books and ebooks are sold.

www.Harlequin.com

JUST CAN'T GET ENOUGH?

Join our social communities
and talk to us online.

You will have access to the latest
news on upcoming titles and special
promotions, but most importantly,
you can talk to other fans about your
favorite Harlequin reads.

Harlequin.com/Community

Facebook.com/HarlequinBooks

Twitter.com/HarlequinBooks

Pinterest.com/HarlequinBooks

HSOCIAL